INDIAN LEADERS

LEADERS ARE BORN, NOT MADE

Dr. Gagan Jain, *D.Litt.*

MGL®

NEW DELHI (INDIA)

INDIAN LEADERS

LEADERS ARE BORN, NOT MADE

This English Edition, Published in India

Published by

MG BOOKS

An Imprint of

MAANU GRAPHICS

MAANU GRAPHICS

(PUBLISHERS OF GENERAL BOOKS)

5FF, Ganpati Bhawan, 21 Ansari Road,
Darya Ganj, New Delhi-110002
Ph: 43755225, 9315898404
E-mail : maanugraphics@yahoo.com
mgbooks.maanu@yahoo.com

Printed at

Satyam Enterprises, Delhi

CONTENTS

AJMAL KHAN

A prominent leader of India's freedom struggle, it was Ajmal Khan who founded the prestigious Jamia Milia Islamia University at Delhi. He is also the sole person who has had the honor to be elected the President of the Indian National Congress, the Muslim League and the All India Khilafat Committee.

Ajmal khan was a prominent freedom fighter, respected physician and academician of India. It was he who founded the prestigious Jamia Milia Islamia University at Delhi.

Ajmal Khan is also the sole person who has had the honor to be elected the President of the Indian National Congress, the Muslim

League and the All India Khilafat Committee.

He was born in the year 1863 at Delhi and belonged from an illustrious family of physicians said to be the lineage in Emperor Babur's army.

Keep reading to know more about the biography of Ajmal Khan. Khan was a religious man who read the holy Quran and other books based on the traditional Islamic knowledge. At the same time, he also studied the medicine at home under the guidance of their family members.

After beginning his practice, Khan was elected as the main physician to the Nawab of Rampur from the time period 1892 to 1902. Here, he was introduced to Syed Ahmed Khan who chose him as the trustee of the Aligarh College, now called the Aligarh Muslim University.

The life history of Ajmal Khan changed its course from medicine towards politics after he started writing for an Urdu weekly 'Akmal-ul-Akhbar' that was launched by his family in 1865-70.

Khan was also heading the Muslim team, who met the Viceroy of India in Shimla in the year 1906 to give him a memorandum made by them.

The following year, he was present at Dhaka when the All India Muslim League was formulated. Dr Ajmal Khan also supported the British during the First World War and asked the Indian to do the same.

At a time when many Muslim leaders were arrested, Dr Ajmal Khan approached Mahatma Gandhi for help. As such, Gandhiji united with him and other Muslim leaders like Maulana Azad, Maulana Mohammad Ali and Maulana Shaukat Ali in the famous Khilafat movement.

Ajmal Khan resigned from the Aligarh Muslim University when the authorities refused to accept the non-cooperation movement waged by Gandhiji and the Congress against the British government. He was elected the president of the Indian National Congress in the year 1921.

ANNIE BESANT

Born Annie Wood, her middle class childhood was marked by economic struggle. Her father died when she was five, and her mother couldn't make ends meet. Friends paid for the education of Annie's brother; Annie was educated at a home school run by a friend of her mother's.

At 19, Annie married the young Rev. Frank Besant, and within four years they had a daughter and a son. Annie's views began to change. She tells in her autobiography that in her role as minister's wife she tried to help her husband's parishioners who were in need, but she came to believe that to alleviate poverty and suffering, deeper social changes were needed beyond immediate service.

Her religious views began to change, too. When she refused to attend communion, her husband ordered her out of their home. They were legally separated, with Frank retaining custody of their son. Annie and her daughter went to London, where Annie soon broke away completely from Christianity, became a freethinker and atheist, and in 1874 joined the Secular Society. Soon, Annie Besant was working for the radical paper, National Reformer, whose editor Charles Bradlaugh was also a leader in the secular (non-religious) movement in England. Together Bradlaugh and Besant wrote a book advocating birth control, which got them a 6-month prison term for "obscene libel."

The sentence was overturned on appeal, and Besant wrote another book advocating birth control, *The Laws of Population*. Publicity denouncing this book led Besant's husband to seek and gain custody of their daughter. During the 1880s Annie Besant continued her activism. She spoke and wrote against unhealthy industrial conditions and low wages for young factory women, in 1888 leading the Match Girls' Strike.

She worked as an elected member of the London School Board for free meals for poor children. She was in demand as a speaker for women's rights, and continued to work for legalization and more available information on birth control. She earned a science degree from London University. And she continued to speak and write defending freethought and atheism and criticizing Christianity.

One pamphlet she wrote, in 1887 with Charles Bradlaugh, "Why I Do Not Believe in God" (reprinted on the web as Part I and Part II) was widely distributed by the secularists and is still considered one of the best summaries of arguments defending atheism. In 1887 Besant converted to Theosophy after meeting

Madame Blavatsky, a spiritualist who in 1875 had founded the Theosophical Society. Besant quickly applied her skills, energy and enthusiasm to this new religious cause.

After Madame Blavatsky died in 1891 at Besant's home, the Theosophical Society split into two branches, with Besant as President of one branch. She was a popular writer and speaker for Theosophy. She often collaborated with Charles Webster Leadbeater in her theosophical writings. Besant moved to India to study Hindu ideas (karma, reincarnation, nirvana) which were foundational to Theosophy. Her Theosophical ideas also brought her to work on behalf of vegetarianism. She returned often to speak for Theosophy or for social reform, remaining active in the British suffrage movement and an important speaker for women's suffrage.

In India, where her daughter and son came to live with her, she worked for Indian Home Rule and was interned during World War I for that activism. She lived in India until her death in Madras in 1933. She was instrumental in establishing Indian National Congress in 1885. A heretic who gave little care to what people thought of her, Annie Besant risked much for her ideas and passionate commitments. From mainline Christianity as a pastor's wife, to radical freethinker, atheist, and social reformer, to Theosophist lecturer and writer, Annie Besant applied her compassion and her logical thinking to the problems of her day, and especially to the problems of women.

ARUNA ASAF ALI

Aruna was born at Kalka, Haryana into a Bengali Brahmo Samaj family. She was educated at Lahore and Nainital. She graduated and worked as a teacher, an achievement in itself for women, given the conditions prevalent in the country at that time. She taught at the Gokhale Memorial School in Calcutta.

She met Asaf Ali, a leader in the congress party at Allahabad and married him in 1928, despite parental opposition on grounds of religion (she was a Hindu while he was a Muslim) and age (a difference of more than 20 years).

She became an active member of Congress Party after marriage and participated in public processions during the Salt Satyagraha. She was arrested on the charge that she was a vagrant and hence not released in 1931 under the Gandhi-Irwin Pact which stipulated release of all political prisoners. Other women co-prisoners refused to leave the premises unless she was also released and gave in only after Mahatma Gandhi intervened. A public agitation secured her release.

In 1932, she was held prisoner at the Tihar Jail where she protested the indifferent treatment of political prisoners by launching a hunger strike. Her efforts resulted in an improvement of conditions in the Tihar Jail but she was moved to Ambala and was subjected to solitary confinement. She was politically not very active after her release.

Her father Upendranath Ganguly hailed from Barisal district of Eastern Bengal but settled in the United Province. He was a restaurant owner and a very adventurous man. Mother Ambalika Devi was the daughter of Trailokyanath Sanyal,a renowned Brahmo leader who wrote many beautiful brahmo hyms. Upendranath Ganguly's younger brother Dhirendranath Ganguly (D G) was one of the earliest film directors.

Another brother Nagendranath, a soil biologist was married to Rabindranath Tagore's only surviving daughter Mira Devi though they got separated after sometime. Her sister, Purnima Banerjee was a member of the Constituent Assembly of India.

On 8 August 1942, the AICC passed the Quit India resolution at the Bombay session. The government responded by arresting the major leaders and all members of the Congress Working Committee and thus tried to pre-empt the movement from success. A young Aruna Asaf Ali presided over the remainder of the session on 9 August and hoisted the Congress flag at the Gowalia Tank maidan.

This marked the commencement of the movement. The police fired upon the assembly at the session. Aruna was dubbed the *Heroine of the 1942 movement* for her bravery in the face of danger and was called *Grand Old Lady of the Independence movement* in her later years. Despite absence of direct leadership, spontaneous protests and demonstrations were held all over the country, as an expression of desire of India's youth to achieve independence.

An arrest warrant was issued in her name but she went underground to evade the arrest. Her property was seized and sold. In the meanwhile, she also edited *Inquilab*, a monthly magazine of the Congress Party, along with Ram Manohar Lohia. In a 1944 issue, she exhorted youth to action by asking them to forget futile discussions about violence and non-violence and join the revolution.

Leaders such as Jayaprakash Narayan and Aruna Asaf Ali were described as *"the Political children of Gandhi but recent students of Karl Marx."* The government announced a reward of Rs. 5,000/- for her capture. She fell ill and Mahatma Gandhi sent her a hand-written note to her to come out of hiding and surrender herself – as her mission was accomplished and as she could utilize the reward amount for the Harijan cause.

However, she came out of hiding only after the warrant against her was withdrawn in 1946. She treasured the note from the Mahatma and it adorned her drawing room. However, she also faced criticism from Gandhi for her support of the RIN Mutiny, a movement she saw as the single greatest unifying factor of Hindus and Muslims at a time that was the peak of the movement for Pakistan.

She was a member of the Congress Socialist Party, a caucus within the Congress Party for activists with socialist leanings. Disillusioned with the progress of Congress party on socialism she joined a new party, Socialist Party in 1948. She however left that party along with Edatata Narayanan and they visited Moscow along with Rajani Palme Dutt. Both of them joined the CPI before Stalin's death.

On domestic front, she was bereaved when Asaf Ali died in 1953. In 1954, she helped form the National Federation of Indian Women, the women's wing of CPI but left the party in 1956 following Khruschev's disowning of Stalin. In 1958, she was elected the first Mayor of Delhi. She and Narayanan started Link publishing house and published a daily, *Patriot* and a weekly, *Link* the same year.

The publications became prestigious due to patronage of leaders such as Nehru, Krishna Menon and Biju Patnaik. Though there was no formal marriage, she and Narayanan practically lived together. Following his death, she moved out of the publishing house due to internal politics, stunned by greed taking over the creed of her comrades. In 1964, she rejoined the Congress Party but stopped taking part in active politics. Despite reservations about the emergency, she remained close to Indira Gandhi and Rajiv Gandhi. She was awarded the Padma Bhushan in her life time.

Aruna Asaf Ali was awarded International Lenin Peace Prize for the year 1964. She was awarded India's highest civilian award, the Bharat Ratna, posthumously in 1997. In 1998, a stamp commemorating her was issued. *Aruna Asaf Ali marg* in New Delhi is named after her. All India Minorities Front distributes the *Dr Aruna Asaf Ali Sadbhawana Award* annually.

ATAL BIHARI VAJPAYEE

ATAL BIHARI VAJPAYEE was born on December 25, 1924 in the erstwhile princely state of Gwalior. He was one of seven children of Shri Krishna Behari, a secondary school teacher and Hindu scholar. Vajpayee graduated from Victoria College (now called Laximbai College) in Gwalior and went on to earn a master's degree in political science from Dayanand Anglo-Vedic (D.A.V.) College in Kanpur.

Vajpayee is a native of Gwalior in Madhya Pradesh state and has been active in Indian politics throughout his adult life. He was one of the founding members of the Bharatiya Jana Sangh, a party linked to the Hindu organisation Rashtriya Swayamsevak Sangh

(RSS), of which he was the president between 1968 and 1973. He was first elected to the Parliament of India in 1957 and was the leader of the Jana Sangh political party up to the formation of the Janata Party in 1977.

He served as the Foreign Minister in the government of Morarji Desai from March 1977 to July 1979. In 1980, he left the Janata Party,and helped form the Bharatiya Janata Party (BJP). He was leader of the BJP parliamentary party between 1980 and 1984, 1986 and between 1993 and 1996. He was the leader of the Opposition in the 11th Lok Sabha.

He was the Prime Minister of India in 1996 and again from 1998 until May 19, 2004. A Hindi poet and an orator, known for his spellbinding eloquence, Vajpayee's first brush with nationalist politics was in his students days when he joined the Quit India Movement of 1942.

A student of political science and law, it was in college that he developed a keen interest in foreign affairs, which he put to skillful use while representing India at various multilateral and bilateral fora. Vajpayee had embarked upon a journalistic career, which was cut short in 1951 when he joined the Bharatiya Jana Sangh. He became the Minister for External Affairs in 1977 when the Janata Party formed the government.

After a third-party coalition governed India between 1996 and 1998, the terribly divided Parliament was dissolved and fresh elections held. These elections again put the BJP at the head. This time, a cohesive bloc of political parties lined up with it to form the National Democratic Alliance, and A.B. Vajpayee was sworn in as the prime minister.

The NDA proved its 286 vote majority in a narrow vote of confidence. Towards the end of 1998 however, the AIADMK under J.Jayalalitha withdrew its support from the 13-month old government. The government lost the ensuing vote of confidence motion by a single vote.

In May 1998, India conducted five underground nuclear weapon tests in Pokhran, Rajasthan. The five tests shocked and surprised the world, especially considering that the government had been in power for only a month. Two weeks later, Pakistan responded with its own nuclear weapon tests, making it the newest nation with nuclear weapons.

While some nations, such as Russia and France, endorsed India's right to defensive nuclear power, others including USA, Canada, Japan, UK and the European Union imposed sanctions on the sale of military equipment and high-tech scientific information, resources and technology to India or Pakistan. In spite of the intense international criticism steady decline in foreign investment and trade, the nuclear tests were popular domestically and the Vajpayee's popularity and the BJP's prestige rose in response.

During his premiership, Vajpayee introduced many important economic and infrastructural reforms domestically including, encouraging the private sector and foreign investements; reducing governmental waste; encouraging research and development and privatizing of government owned corporations.

On October 13, 1999, he took charge as the Prime Minister of India for the second consecutive term as the head of a new coalition government - the National Democratic Alliance. He has completed his tenure of 5 years as the Prime Minister of India. Now, he is one of the most respected political leaders of India.

AUROBINDO GHOSE

He was a freedom fighter, poet, scholar, yogi and philosopher. Worked towards the cause of India's freedom, and for further evolution of life on earth.

Aurobindo Ghose was a multifaceted person. He was a freedom fighter, poet, scholar, yogi and philosopher. He spent his life working towards the cause of India's freedom, and for further evolution of life on earth.

Sri Aurobindo Ghosh was born on August 15, 1872 at Calcutta. His father was Krishnadhan and his mother was Swamalata. Aurobindo Ghose had an impressive lineage.

Raj Narayan Bose, an acknowledged leader in Bengali literature, and the grandfather of Indian nationalism was Sri Aurobindo's maternal grandfather. Aurobindo Ghosh owes not only his rich spiritual nature, but even his very superior literary capacity, to his mother's line. His father was an M.D. from England.

When Sri Aurobindo was five years old, he was sent to Loretto Convent School at Darjeeling. Two years later in 1879, Aurobindo Ghose, was sent to England along with his brothers for higher studies. Aurobindo completed his schooling from St. Paul's in London. In 1890, at the age of eighteen, Sri Aurobindo got admission into Cambridge.

Here, he distinguished himself as a student of European classics. To comply with the wish of his father, Sri Aurobindo Ghose also applied for the ICS while at Cambridge. He passed the Indian Civil Service Examination with great credit in 1890.

He, however, failed to stand the required test in horsemanship and hence was not allowed to enter the Covenantal Service of the Indian Government. In 1893, Aurobindo Ghose, returned to India, and became the Vice-principal of the State college in Baroda. He drew a salary of Rs.750/-.

He was held in great respect by the Maharaja of Baroda. Aurobindo was an accomplished scholar in Greek and Latin. From 1893 to 1906 he extensively studied Sanskrit, Bengali literature, Philosophy and Political Science. In 1906, in the wake of partition of Bengal, resigned his job and joined the Bengal National College on a salary of Rs.150/-.

He plunged headlong into the revolutionary movement. Aurobindo Ghose played a leading role in India's freedom struggle from 1908. Sri Aurobindo Ghosh was one of the pioneers of political awakening in India.

He edited the English daily Bande Mataram and wrote fearless and pointed editorials. He openly advocated the boycott of British goods, British courts and everything British.

He asked the people to prepare themselves for passive resistance.The famous Alipore Bomb Case proved to be a turning point in Sri Aurobindo Ghosh's life.

For a year Aurobindo was an undertrial prisoner in solitary confinement in the Alipore Central Jail. It was in a dingy cell of the Alipore Jail that he dreamt the dream of his future life, the divine mission ordained for him by God.

He utilized this period of incarceration for an intense study and practice of the teachings of the Bhagavad Gita. Chittaranjan Das defended Sri Aurobindo, who was acquitted after a memorable trial.

During his time in prison, Aurobindo Ghosh, had developed interest in yoga and meditation.

After his release he started practicing pranayama and meditation. Sri Aurobindo Ghose migrated from Calcutta to Pondicherry in 1910. At Pondicherry, he stayed at a friend's place. At first, he lived there with four or five companions.

Gradually the number of members increased and an Ashram was founded. In 1914 after four years of concentrated yoga at Pondicherry, Sri Aurobindo launched Arya, a 64 page monthly review. For the next six and a half years this became the vehicle for most of his most important writings, which appeared in serialised form.

These included Essays on The Gita, The Secret of The Veda, Hymns to the Mystic Fire, The Upanishads, The Foundations of Indian Culture, War and Self-determination, The Human Cycle,

The Ideal of Human Unity, and The Future Poetry. In 1926, Sri Aurobindo Ghose retired from public life.

Sri Aurobindo's philosophy is based on facts, experience and personal realisations and on having the vision of a seer or Rishi. Aurobindo's spirituality was inseparably united with reason.

The goal of Sri Aurobindo was not merely the liberation of the individual from the chain that fetters him and realization of the self, but to work out the will of the Divine in the world, to effect a spiritual transformation and to bring down the divine nature and a divine life into the mental, vital and physical nature and life of humanity. Sri Aurobindo passed away on December 5, 1950 at Pondicherry at the age of 78.

BAL GANGADHAR TILAK

BAL GANGADHAR TILAK was a great Sanskrit scholar and astronomer. He fixed the origin and date of Rigvedic Aryans, which was highly acclaimed and universally accepted by orientalists of his time.

His role in Congress and advocating Home Rule for India were enormous. His newspaper (Kesari) founded in 1881 is going strong even today. He was Guru to V.D. Savarkar and hundreds of nationalists and thousands of Indians.

He led the Indian Freedom Movement, till 1920, his death. After him Gandhiji took over. Although Gandhi accepted Gokhale as his mentor, in practice, he adopted all of Tilak's ideas of Swadeshi and of social reform.

His words, "Swaraj is my birthright and I shall have it!" roused a sleeping nation to action, making Indian people aware of their political plight under a foreign rule. Tilak did not question the British Sovereignty nor his demands were rebellious or revolutionary. All he was asking was favorable conditions in India, to enable people to learn to govern themselves.

May be all over the world, the separatist forces should follow his vision and define freedom as ability to govern one's land. But the handful rulers who ruled India's millions thought otherwise. They thought that Tilak was whipping a rebellion and he was imprisoned twice; two years for the first and six during the second. They said, he had committed treason.

Born in Ratnagiri, a small coastal town in 1856 in a middle class family, Tilak had to feed himself for college education. At an early age he was convinced that the educational system the British provided for the Indians was not at all adequate.

After graduation and a law degree, he helped found a school which laid emphasis on nationalism. He started a news paper 'Kesari' which tried to teach Indians of their glorious past and reminded them to be self reliant (Swadeshi).

Tilak rightly calculated the attitude of the British towards the economic exploitation of the Indians. The British used the raw material from the Indian soil and produced finished products in their country, which in turn were sold in India. This made the Indians totally dependent on the British.

In the process, all the self-employing industries of India like spinning, weaving, glass making, sugar ,dyeing, paper making were destroyed. People became destitute for no fault of theirs to help an empire become richer and stronger.

To fight this situation, he gave four mantras called Chatuhsutri: (1). Boycott of foreign goods (2) National Education (3) Self Government (4) Swadeshi or self reliance. He realized that mere protest against British rule was not going to help and insisted on native production and reliance.

He founded Deccan Education Society to give better education as per the country's needs. He wrote articles over inhuman punishment meted out to the nationalist youth who protested the division of Bengal (VangaBhanga).

Indian newspapers were not to criticize the British policy in those days and two articles titled "Has the Government lost its head ?" and "To Rule is not to wreak vengeance" appearing in Kesari landed him in jail, after a namesake trial.

For the first time in British history, intellectuals in England (including the great orientalist, Max Muller) were able to convince the Government that the trial was unfair. But the second time (1908) was no different.

Tilak advocated his own case and when the judgment of six years of black-waters (kala pani) imprisonment was pronounced, he gave the famous statement :

" All I wish to say is that in spite of the verdict of the jury, I maintain my innocence. There are higher powers that rule the destiny of men and nations. It may be the will of Providence that the cause I represent may prosper by suffering than by remaining free"

His trial and punishment led to national upheaval. But the British were careful enough to arrange everything in secret and the judgment was delivered at midnight and Tilak was taken under military vigil to be deported to Burma (present Myanmar, which was also under British control).

At 52, Tilak wrote his famous commentary on Bhagavad-Gita, the sacred book of Hindus; Geeta-Rahasya in the jail. By the time Tilak completed his six year prison term, he was the unquestioned leader of the Indians - the uncrowned king. He was known as the Tilak Maharaj.

There was unprecedented jubilation after Tilak was free and back in India. Civil resistance, the concept of Swaraj, and nationalism had taken deep roots. Tilak's suffering did not go in vain. A band of leaders, full of zeal for nationalism and self-sacrifice was coming up.

National schools were coming up in all corners of India. He paved the way for Khadi (hand woven cloth), picketing against foreign goods and alcoholism. His death in 1920 brought Mahatma Gandhi on the scene and Gandhiji gave a concrete shape to Tilak's ideas of Swadeshi.

BIPIN CHANDRA PAL

The only son of his parents, Bipin Chandra Pal took his early education from a Maulvi in Sylhet town. He had his formal education at Sylhet Government High School from where he passed the Entrance Examination. He then got himself admitted in the Presidency College, but gave up his studies before graduating. His literary competence was, however, remarkable and he studied the *Gita* and the *Upanishad*s extensively.

Pal started his career in early 1879 as a Headmaster of a High School and served in this capacity in different schools in and outside Sylhet. For sometime (1890-91) he worked as the librarian and secretary of the Calcutta Public Library. While in Calcutta during his student life, he came in close contact with some prominent personalities like keshab chandra sen, shibnath shastri and Bijoy Krishna Goswami.

Under the influence of Keshab Chandra Sen he was attracted to the Brahma movement. Bijoy Krishna Goswami also tremendously influenced his spiritual ideas. His association with Sivanath Sastri made him conscious of the spirit of social revolt and patriotism.

Surendranath Banerje inspired Bipin Pal to take part in active politics. Soon, however, he became a convert to the extremist ideas of BG Tilak, Lajpat Rai and aurobinda ghosh, though he could not accept Tilak's concept of Hindu nationalism. He was an exponent of 'composite patriotism' which, he thought, was suitable for a country like India.

Bipin Chandra Pal was connected with the progressive force of the Congress since 1885 and attended the second and the third annual sessions of the Congress held in Calcutta and Madras in 1886 and 1887 respectively. He compelled the Congress to take up the cause of the Assam Tea-garden labourers who were cruelly treated by the planters.

Bipin Pal went to study comparative theology in England in 1898 but after a year came back to India and started preaching the ideal of *Swaraj* (complete independence) through his weekly journal the *New India*. Imbued with great patriotic zeal, he devoted himself to the freedom movement of India.

He presided over the Bombay session of the indian national congress in 1904. Following the partition of bengal, 1905, Bipin Pal started a daily paper the *Bande Mataram* and became its chief editor. He firmly stood against the partition of Bengal on the ground that it was a calculated move of the government to split the Bengalis and thus to break their growing political influence.

With a view to enlisting the mass support behind the anti-partition campaign, Bipin Pal, along with other anti-partitionists, organised propaganda tour in various parts of Bengal, Assam, UP and Madras.

Pal was one of the architects of the swadeshi movement, which swept over India during the days following the partition of Bengal. He suffered imprisonment for six months in 1907 for his refusal to give evidence against Aurovinda Ghosh in the so-called Bande Mataram Sedition Case.

On his release, Pal went to England in 1908 'to lead the life of an enforced exile' and stayed there for three years. After the First World War, he visited England for the third time in 1919 as a member of the Home Rule League deputation led by Tilak. He presided over the Bengal Provincial Conference held at Barisal in 1921.

He did not involve in the non-cooperation movement because it was merged with the Khilafat cause and criticised the bengal pact (1923) of chitta ranjan das. He could not share the views of Maulana Mohammad Ali on the nature of the communal problem in India (1920-25). From 1925 onward, he, however, retired from active politics.

Bipin Chandra Pal encouraged journalism and started the Bangla weekly *Paridarshak* in Sylhet (1886). He worked as Assistant Editor of the *Bengali Public Opinion* (1882) and served the *Lahore Tribune* for a short time (1887).

For sometime he was the editor of *The Democrat* and *The Independent*. He published a biography (in Bangla) of Queen Victoria in 1887. Among his other books *Indian Nationalism*, *Nationality and Empire*,

Swaraj and the Present Situation, *The Basis of Social Reform*, *The Soul of India*, *The New Spirit* and *Studies in Hinduism* are prominent.

A man of undaunted spirit, Bipin Chandra Pal made no compromise in the sphere of politics when it was a question of conviction and conscience. He revolted against the evils and abuses of the Hindu society at a very early stage of his life. He championed the cause of Indian education with special emphasis on female education and advocated the equality of male and female.

Being a member of the Brahma Samaj, he married Nrityakali Devi, a Brahmin widow. After her death, he was married to another Brahmin widow, Birajmohini Devi, a distant relation of Surendranath Banerjea.

A renowned orator, Bipin Chandra Pal inspired his audience during the Indian nationalist movements. He occupies a unique place in the history of the freedom movement of India. He died in Calcutta in 1932.

CHAKRAVARTI RAJAGOPALACHARI

Chakravarthi Rajagopalachari (December 1878 - December 25, 1972), known as or Rajaji or C.R., was an Indian lawyer, writer, statesman and a Hindu spiritualist. He was the second Governor-General of independent India. Later he became the Chief Minister of the Madras Presidency.

At one time considered Mahatma Gandhi's heir, this brilliant lawyer from Salem was regarded in pre-independence years as one of the top five leaders of the Congress along with Jawaharlal Nehru, Rajendra Prasad, Sardar Vallabhai Patel, and Maulana

Abdul Kalam Azad. Of the five, Rajaji, Nehru and Patel were christened the "head, heart and hands" of Gandhi, in whose shadows they remained till his death.

Ironically, all three of them were to have a tempestuous relationship, bound together only by their common goal and Gandhi's charm. However, they respected each other immensely. Nehru wrote about Rajaji in his autobiography of how Rajaji's "brilliant intellect, selfless character, and penetrating powers of analysis have been a tremendous asset to our cause".

Rajaji was perhaps the earliest Congress leader in the forties to admit to the likelihood of Partition. He even prophesied then, that Pakistan might break up in twenty-five years.

Rajaji was known to be a fierce defendant of his political ideals, and did not hesitate to contradict his closest aides and friends in public, whenever he sensed a threat to them. Later, C.R. became a strident critic of Nehru and the Congress. As a founder of the Swatantra party in the fifties, he attacked the 'permit-license Raj' fearing its potential for corruption and stagnation, even while the tide was in favour of Nehru's socialistic pattern.

He wrote in his newspaper Swarajya thus -

"Encouraging competition in industry and giving incentives for higher production are good for the public as well as for the private interests.

I want an India where talent and energy can find scope for play without having to cringe and obtain special individual permission from officials and ministers, and where their efforts will be judged by the open market in India and abroad. [...]

I want the inefficiency of public management to go where the competitive economy of private management can look after affairs. [...] I want the corruptions of the permit-license-raj to go. [...] I want the officials appointed to administer laws and policies to be free from pressures of the bosses of the ruling party, and gradually restored back to the standards of fearless honesty which they once maintained. [...] I want real equal opportunities for all and no private monopolies created by the permit-license- raj. [...] I want the money power of big business to be isolated from politics. [...] I want an India where dharma once again rules the hearts of men and not greed."

Decades later, in 1991, India shifted from the Nehruvian system to globalization through economic reforms.

The bureaucratic barriers imposed on the pretext of protecting Indian interests, have been gradually removed, and the economy has since made rapid strides, quickly achieving one of the highest growth rates in the world. Since then, many political critics have reaffirmed Rajaji's image as a visionary, whose vast intellect and was under-utilized and neglected, for political reasons.

After serving time in British prisons for his work in Gandhi's independence movement, he became a member of the Governor's Council in 1946. In 1948, after Indian independence was attained, he replaced Mountbatten, becoming the only Indian Governor-General of India, serving until 1950.

When a government was installed with the new constitution of January 26, 1950, the office was replaced that of President, first held by Rajendra Prasad.

Rajaji became a member of Jawaharlal Nehru's cabinet, first without portfolio, then as Minister for Home Affairs. He was chief minister of Madras from 1952 to 1954. On leaving government, he was among the first recipients of the Bharat Ratna, the Indian government's highest civilian award.

Rajaji was also a profound thinker, in matters of spirituality and religion. A popular anecdote recalls his encounter with the Hindu spiritaul leader Swami Vivekananda, during his student days.

Swami was visiting a student hostel where Rajaji was staying, and he drew the attention of the inmates of the hostel to a painting of Lord Vishnu hanging over the wall and asked them as to why Vishnu in all his images, was always depicted blue in colour ?

Rajaji showed some amazing intellect by answering that the Lord has been ascribed the color of the infinite sky and the unlimited sea, which were both blue in colour. Rajaji received rich praises from the immensely pleased spiritual leader, for his profound understanding of the Hindu spiritual philosophy.

As a writer, besides his own material, he published English translations of many important Indian and Hindu works: Ramayana, Mahabharata, Bhagavad Gita, Upanishads and Bhaja Govindam. He also translated the Ramayana into Tamil.

Kurai Onrum illai (meaning - I have no unfulfilled desires left, oh! God) is a very famous song in the semi-Carnatic music genre written by Rajaji and the most popular version, (widely acknowledged as soul-stirring) has been rendered by MS Subbulakshmi.

Rajaji died in December, 1972 after a short illness. The nonagenarian's public life, spanning nearly eighty years are perhaps best recognized by Mahatma Gandhi's rich tribute to him praising him as the: "the keeper of my conscience".

DR. BHIMRAO AMBEDKAR

DR. BHIMRAO AMBEDKAR, the fourteenth of Ramji and Bhimabai Sakpal Ambavedkar, was born on April 14, 1891, in Mhow, Central India into the "untouchable" Mahar caste. His father, and grandfather Maloji, were in the British Army. The Government required all Army personnel and their families to be educated and ran schools for this purpose. Thus the Sakpal family was fortunate to receive good education which otherwise, would have been denied to them.

Bhim began to taste the bitter reality of being born "untouchable" in school. He had to sit on the floor in one corner in the classroom.

Teachers would not touch his notebooks. If Bhim felt thirsty, he could only drink water if someone else poured water into his mouth.

Once provoked by an uncontrollable fit of thirst, Bhim drank from the public reservoir. He was found out and beaten by the higher caste Hindus. These experiences were permanently etched onto his mind. He realized that this was the plight of anyone born "untouchable."

While in school, Bhim's teacher Ambedkar, entered his last name into the school records as Ambedkar. Teacher Ambedkar and Pendse, were the only ones in the entire school who were kind and affectionate to young him. They made the few fond memories Dr. B.R. Ambedkar had of his school days.

Bhim enrolled in the Elphinstone High School in Bombay. Even there, one of his teachers constantly mocked him, saying that of what use was an educated Mahar. Bhim swallowed these insults and controlled his anger. He passed his matriculation examination in 1907. The Mahar community felicitated him on his achievement.

Bhim joined the Elphinstone College for further education. After completing his Intermediate course, Bhim received a scholarship from the Maharaja of Baroda, Sayaji Rao, and attained a Bachelors in Arts in 1912. The February of next year, Bhim father and mentor, Ramji died.

Sayaji Rao selected Bhim to be sent to America on a scholarship for higher studies. In return, Bhim Rao would have to serve the State of Baroda for ten years. Bhim Rao reached New York in July 1913. For the first time in his life, Bhim Rao was not demeaned for being a Mahar.

He put his heart into his studies and received a degree in Master of Arts and a Doctorate in Philosophy from Columbia University in 1916 for his thesis "National Dividend for India: A Historical and Analytical Study."

From America, Bhim Rao proceeded to London to study economics and political science. The Government of Baroda terminated his scholarship and recalled him to Baroda. Bhim Rao vowed to return to London to complete his studies.

The Maharaj appointed him to the post of Military Secretary but who cared to take orders from an "untouchable" Mahar. Bhim Rao could not even get lodging and not even the Prime Minister appointed by the Maharaja could help Bhim Rao find a place to live. Bhim Rao returned to Bombay in November 1917. and took a part time job in the Sydenham College with the sole aim of going to London to complete his studies.

With the help of Shahu Maharaj of Kolhapur, a sympathizer of the cause for the upliftment of the depressed classes, Bhim Rao started a fortnightly newspaper, the Mooknayak (Leader of the Dumb) on January 31, 1920.

The Maharaj also convened many meeting and conferences of the "untouchables" which Bhim Rao addressed. Impressed by Ambedkar, the Maharaj declared at a meeting, "You have found your saviour in Ambedkar. I am confident he will break your shackles."

In September 1920, after accumulating sufficient funds, Ambedkar returned to London to complete his studies. He became a barrister and got a Doctorate in Science. He now considered himself fully equipped to fight the evil of "untouchability."

In July 1924, Ambedkar founded the Bahishkrut Hitkaraini Sabha. The aim of the Sabha was to uplift the downtrodden socially and politically and bring them to the level of the others in the Indian society.

The Sabha aimed at scrapping the caste system from the Hindu religion. The Sabha started free school for the young and the old and ran reading rooms and libraries. Dr. Ambedkar took the grievances of the "untouchables" to court and gave them justice. Soon he became a father-figure to the poor and downtrodden and was respectfully called "Babasaheb."

On March 19-20, 1927 a conference of the depressed classes was held at Mahad. Ten thousand delegates attended, workers and leaders attended. Babasaheb condemned the British for banning the recruitment of "untouchables" into the military. He declared,

"No lasting progress can achieved unless we put ourselves through a threefold process of purification. We must improve the general tone of our demeanor, re-tone our pronunciation and revitalize our thoughts. I, therefore, ask you now to take a vow to renounce eating carrion, the... flesh of... animals, from this moment. ...Make an unflinching resolve not to eat the thrown away crumbs. We will attain self-elevation only if we learn self-help, regain our self respect and gain self-knowledge."

The next day, the conference decided to implement the resolution passed 4 years ago to open public places to all regardless of religion, caste or creed by drinking from the Chavdar Taley (Sweet-water Tank). They walked to the tank and drank from its water. Higher caste Hindus attacked them.

They beat the delegates, pulled down the conference pulpit, threw away all the cooked food and broke all the vessels. Ambedkar told his people to stay calm and not to retaliate. Later the Hindus performed rituals to "purify" the "defiled" water. Ambedkar vowed to offer a satyagraha and re- establish his peoples right over the water tank.

On December 25 of the same year, thousands responded to Ambedkar's call. Speaker after speaker spoke, passions rose and the vast gathering waited for the satyagraha to begin with intense anticipation. The satyagraha was deferred when the matter was referred to the court. At the end of conference, a copy of the Manusmruti, the age-old code of the Hindus that gave rise to the caste system, was ceremoniously burnt. In a thundering voice, Ambedkar demanded in its place a new smruti, devoid of all social stratification. This act sent shockwaves through the nation.

When a separate electorate was announced for the depressed classes, Gandhiji went on a fast unto death against this decision. Leaders rushed to Dr. Ambedkar to drop the demand for a separate electorate.

Ambedkar held fast and did not buckle under the immense pressure. Finally on September 24, 1932, Ambedkar and Gandhiji signed the Poona Pact. According to the pact the separate electorate demand was replaced with special concessions like reserved seats in the regional legislative assemblies and Central Council of States.

On May 27, 1935, Dr. Ambedkar's wife Ramabai died. Ambedkar could not bear the loss of his wife. He broke down, a shattered man. On October 13, 1935, at a conference at Nasik, Dr. Ambedkar reviewed the progress made on the condition of the "untouchables" in the decade since Ambedkar started his agitation. Ambedkar declared that their efforts had not borne the kind of results he had expected.

He then made a fantastic appeal to the "untouchables." He encouraged them to forsake the Hindu religion and convert to a religion where they would be treated with equality. The nation was shocked.

A clause of an agrarian bill referred to the depressed classes as "Harijans," or people of God. Ambedkar was strongly opposed to this title for the untouchables. He argued that if the "untouchables" were people of God then all others would be people of monsters. He was against any such reference. But the Indian National Congress succeeded in introducing the term Harijan.

Ambedkar felt bitter that they could not have any say in what they were called. On July 15, 1947, the British Parliament passed the act of Indian Independence and on August 15, 1947, India became free. The Constituent Assemble of Independent India appointed a Drafting Committee with Dr. Ambedkar as its Chairman to draft the Constitution of India.

Dr. Ambedkar was also invited to join the Cabinet as the Minister of Law. Ambedkar toiled over the Constitution while he took care of his ministry. In February 1948, Dr. Ambedkar presented the Draft Constitution before the people of India.

The mammoth effort had taken its toll on Dr. Ambedkar's health. He went to Bombay for treatment and married Dr. Sharada Kabir on April 15, 1948, who worked in the same hospital where he was receiving treatment.

The Constituent Assemble adopted the Draft Constitution as the Constitution of India on November 26, 1949 with all its 356 Articles and eight Schedules and Article 11 which abolished untouchability in all forms.

In October 1948, Dr. Ambedkar submitted the Hindu Code Bill to the Constituent Assembly in an attempt to codify the Hindu law. The Bill caused great divisions even in the Congress party. Consideration for the bill was postponed to September 1951. When the Bill was taken up it was truncated. A dejected Ambedkar relinquished his position as Law Minister.

In May 1956, on Buddha's Anniversary, Dr. Ambedkar announced that on October 14 he would embrace Buddhism. With him his wife and some three lakh followers also converted to the faith. When asked why, Dr. Ambedkar replied, "Why can't you ask this question to yourself and... your forefathers...?"

On December 5, 1956, Dr. Bhim Rao Ambedkar died peacefully in his sleep or as the Buddhists would say, he attained "nirvana."

DR. DADABHAI NAOROJI

Dadabhai Naoroji was born in Bombay on 4th September 1825, the son of Maneckbai and Naoroji Palanji Dordi, a poor Athornan (priestly) Parsi family.

At the age of 4, Dadabhai's father died and his mother was left the difficult task of bringing up the family, and she managed admirably. According to prevailing customs, she arranged the marriage of Dadabhai to Gulbai at the early age of 11. For the rest of her life, Maneckbai remained a close companion and mentor to Dadabhai.

"She made me what I am" noted Dadabhai in 1901 when he gave an account of his early life in "The Days of my Youth."

Dadabhai became a scholar at the Elphinstone Institution (now Elphinstone College, Bombay) and had a brilliant academic career.

In 1850 at the early age of 25, he was appointed Assistant Professor, and 4 years later, Professor of Mathematics and Natural Philosophy at the Elphinstone Institution.

Professor Orlebar of the college called him "The Promise of India". Dadabhai, being an Athornan (ordained priest), founded the Rahnumae Mazdayasne Sabha (Guides on the Mazdayasne Path) on 1st August 1851.

The ethos of the Rahnumae at its inception was to restore the Zoroastrian religion to its original purity and simplicity. The society is still in operation in Bombay.

On 27th June 1855, Dadabhai sailed for England to join the first Indian business firm of the mercantile Cama family. In 1859, Dadabhai established his own business firm under the name of Dadabhai Naoroji & Co.

On 31st October 1861, an association was founded in the name of "THE LONDON ANJUMAN" and Dr. Dadabhai Naoroji was its Patron, Founder and First President.

During his time in England, Dadabhai endeavored to educate the British people about their responsibilities as rulers of India.

He delivered speeches and published articles to support his opposition to the unjust and oppressive regime of the British Raj.

In 1867 he helped to establish the East India Association of which he became the Honorary Secretary.

'he purpose of the Association was to keep Britain well informed f India's plight and needs and to secure fair treatment for India's eople.

'his was his first political move and his colleagues were not slow 1 realizing his aspirations, echoing Professor Orlebar's sentiment s "The Promise of India".

)adabhai presented to the British people the "Drain Theory", 'hich put before them the facts and figures illustrating systematic leeding of the wealth and resources of India. His ideas were put 1to a volume called "Poverty and UnBritish rule in India".

'his was a charge against the British Empire, and he asked for nmediate appointment of a Royal Commission to look into the harges. Dadabhai was one of the members of the Royal ;ommission.

)adabhai went back to India in 1869 but soon returned to England) give evidence before the Parliamentary Commission on Indian 'inance. Dadabhai returned to India in 1874, having been ppointed Dewan of Baroda State.

Ie came back to England in 1886 with the idea of getting into 1e British Parliament to enable him to fight from within the ystem, and further the cause of his native country India.

)adabhai was elected to Parliament on the 5th of July 1892 and ntered the House of Commons as a Liberal, representing the ;entral Finsbury constituency.

Ie delivered his maiden speech in the House of Commons in ugust 1892. This was indeed a historic occasion as Dadabhai Iaoroji became the first ever Indian/Asian Member of the British 'arliament.

Dadabhai immediately championed various causes in the Hous of Commons. He made many speeches both in England and ii India on political reforms, fair play and justice for India,whicl spearheaded the beginning of the freedom struggle. He wa renowned as the founding father of Indian Nationalism.

Dadabhai's success on being elected to the Parliament wa followed by two other Indian Parsi Zoroastrians; Sir Muncherje Merwanji Bhownagree and Sir Sorabji Saklatvala.

Dadabhai's reputation and his help facilitated the political career of both these gentlemen.

Dadabhai was one of the moving spirits and founder of the India National Congress. He took part in the inauguration of the India National Congress that was held in Bombay in 1865, before hi departure to England. Dadabhai was thrice elected President o the Congress.

Dadabhai Naoroji had attempted to keep the Freedom movemen on a moderate path during the formative years of the Congress He had put his faith in the British.

He believed that if they were informed of India's problems, they would reform their method of rule. However, his experience o the British political system and years of dealing with Britisl officialdom led to increasing disillusionment.

Dadabhai began to despair when even moderate claims were no considered. In 1904 Dadabhai demanded "SWARAJ" Sel Government for India.

Dadabhai said "Indians were British citizens with a birthright tc be free" and that they had "every right to claim an honorabl fulfillment of our British pledged rights". -"It is futile to tell m that we must ait till all the people are ready.

The British people did not -wait for their parliament". "Self-government is the only and chief remedy. In self-government is our hope, strength and greatness".

'I am a Hindu, a Muslim, a Parsi, but above all an Indian First".On 1st September 1888, Gandhi sailed from Bombay with a letter of introduction to Dadabhai.

Mahatma Gandhi wrote "...you will, therefore oblige me greatly if you will kindly direct and guide me and make necessary suggestions which shall be received as from a father to his child". Gandhi further wrote:

'The story of a life so noble and yet so simple needs no introduction from me or anybody else. May it be an inspiration to the readers even as Dadabhai living was to me". "And so Dadabhai became real DADA to me".

The Grand Old Man of India once asked "Is it vanity that I should take great pleasure in being hailed as the Grand Old Man of India?

No, that title, which speaks volumes for the warm, grateful and generous hearts of my countrymen, is to me, whether I deserve it or not, the highest reward of my life".

A great life nobly lived, spanning nearly a whole century, great, indeed in the greatness of its simplicity, purity and benignity and lofty in its concept of man's mission on earth, came to an end on 30th June 1917.

Dadabhai passed away at the ripe old age of 93.

DR. MANMOHAN SINGH

Dr. Manmohan Singh is an Indian politician, economist academician and bureaucrat who served as the 14th Prime Minister of India from 2004 to 2014. He is the third longest-serving prime minister after Jawaharlal Nehru and Indira Gandhi. A member of the Indian National Congress, Singh was the first Sikh and non Hindu prime minister of India. He was also the first prime minister since Jawaharlal Nehru to be re-elected after completing a full five-year term.

Dr. Manmohan Singh is rightly acclaimed as a thinker and a scholar He is well regarded for his diligence and his academic approach to work, as well as his accessibility and his unassuming demeanour.

Dr. Manmohan Singh was born on September 26, 1932, in a village in the Punjab province of undivided India. Dr. Singh completed his Matriculation examinations from the Panjab University in 1948. His academic career took him from Punjab to the University of Cambridge, UK, where he earned a First Class Honours degree in Economics in 1957.

Dr. Singh followed this with a D.Phil in Economics from Nuffield College at Oxford University in 1962. His book, "India's Export Trends and Prospects for Self-Sustained Growth" was an early critique of India's inward-oriented trade policy.

Dr. Singh's academic credentials were burnished by the years he spent on the faculty of Punjab University and the prestigious Delhi School of Economics.

He had a brief stint at the UNCTAD Secretariat as well, during these years. This presaged a subsequent appointment as Secretary General of the South Commission in Geneva between 1987 and 1990.

In 1971, Dr. Singh joined the Government of India as Economic Advisor in the Commerce Ministry. This was soon followed by his appointment as Chief Economic Advisor in the Ministry of Finance in 1972. Among the many Governmental positions that Dr. Singh has occupied are Secretary in the Ministry of Finance; Deputy Chairman of the Planning Commission; Governor of the Reserve Bank of India; Advisor of the Prime Minister; and Chairman of the University Grants Commission.

In what was to become the turning point in the economic history of independent India, Dr. Singh spent five years between 1991 and 1996 as India's Finance Minister.

His role in ushering in a comprehensive policy of economic reforms is now recognized worldwide. In the popular view of those years in India, that period is inextricably associated with the persona of Dr. Singh.

Among the many awards and honours conferred upon Dr. Singh in his public career, the most prominent are India's second highest civilian honour, the Padma Vibhushan (1987); the Jawaharlal Nehru Birth Centenary Award of the Indian Science Congress (1995); the Asia Money Award for Finance Minister of the Year (1993 and 1994); the Euro Money Award for Finance Minister of the Year (1993), the Adam Smith Prize of the University of Cambridge (1956); and the Wright's Prize for Distinguished Performance at St. John's College in Cambridge (1955). Dr. Singh has also been honoured by a number of other associations including by the Japanese Nihon Keizai Shimbun.

Dr. Singh has represented India at many international conferences and in several international organizations. He has led Indian Delegations to the Commonwealth Heads of Government Meeting in Cyprus (1993) and to the World Conference on Human Rights in Vienna in 1993.

In his political career, Dr. Singh has been a Member of India's Upper House of Parliament (the Rajya Sabha) since 1991, where he was Leader of the Opposition between 1998 and 2004.

Singh served as Governor of the Reserve Bank of India from 1982 to 1985, and was hand picked as finance minister in cabinet of then Prime Minister Narasimha Rao in 1991.

Singh became leader of opposition in uppder house of Indian Parliament, and stayed with the Congress Partyduring a major split in 1999, when three senior Congress leaders objected to Sonia Gandhi's rise as Congress President.

Being touted as the Congress choice for the PM's job, Gandhi had become a target of nationalists who objected to her Italian birth.

An alliance led by the Congress Party won a surprisingly high number of seats in the Parliamentary elections of 2004. The Left Front decided to support a coalition government led by the Congress Party from the outside.

Sonia Gandhi was elected leader of the Congress Parliamentary Party and was expected to become the Prime Minister. In a surprise move, she declined to accept the post and instead nominated Dr. Singh.

He secured the nomination for prime minister on May 19, 2004 when the then President A.P.J. Abdul Kalam officially asked him to form a government. Although most expected him to head the Finance Ministry himself, he entrusted the job to P. Chidambaram.

His appointment is notable as it comes 20 years after India witnessed significant tensions between the Indian central government and the Punjabi Sikh community.

After Congress Party Prime Minister Indira Gandhi, the mother-in-law of Sonia Gandhi, ordered central government troops to storm the Golden Temple (the holiest site of Sikhism) in Amritsar, Punjab to quell a separatist movement, she was assassinated by her Sikh bodyguards.

Singh's image is generally regarded as intellectual, honest but cautious, attentive to working class people (on whose votes he was elected), and technocratic.

Although legislative achievements have been few and the Congress-led alliance is routinely hampered by conflicts, Singh's administration has focused on reducing the fiscal deficit, providing debt-relief to poor farmers, extending social programs and advancing the pro-industry economic and tax policies that have launched the country on a major economic expansion course since 2002.

Singh has been the image of the Congress campaign to defuse religious tensions and conflicts and bolster political support from minorities like Muslims, Christians and Sikhs.

The Prime Minister's foreign policy has been to continue the new peace process with Pakistan initiated by his predecessor, Atal Bihari Vajpayee. Exchange visits by top leaders from both countries have highlighted this year, as has reduced terrorism and increased prosperity in the state of Kashmir.

His government has endeavored to build stronger relations with the United States, the People's Republic of China and European nations.

The Government suffered a setback when it lost the support of a key ally, several African Union members, for its bid for a permanent membership to the U.N. Security Council with veto privileges.

One of the biggest achievements of Manmohan Singh's Government has been a nuclear deal between India and the U.S.A. Under Dr. Singh, an economist and Finance minister P. Chidambaram, India's economic growth has continued, with the GDP growing at a very fast rate. This has resulted in India becoming a trillion dollar economy.

Dr. Singh and his wife Mrs. Gursharan Kaur have three daughters.

Dr. Singh visited China on 14th January, 2008 and extended successfully friendship and trade economy with that country.

DR. RAJENDRA PRASAD

Dr. Rajendra Prasad was the first President of independent India. He was the President of the Constituent Assembly that drafted the Constitution. He had also served as a Cabinet Minister briefly in the first Government of independent India. Dr. Rajendra Prasad was one of the foremost disciples of Gandhiji and he played a crucial role in Indian freedom struggle.

Dr. Rajendra Prasad was born on December 3, 1884 in Ziradei village in Siwan district of Bihar. His father's name was Mahadev Sahay and his mother's name was Kamleshwari Devi. Rajendra Prasad was youngest among his siblings. Mahadev Sahay was a

Persian and Sanskrit language scholar. Dr. Rajendra Prasad was greatly attached to his mother and elder brother Mahendra.

At the age of five Rajendra Prasad was, according to the practice in the community to which he belonged, put under a Maulavi who taught him Persian. Later, he was taught Hindi and arithmetic. At the age of 12, Rajendra Prasad was married to Rajvanshi Devi.

Dr. Rajendra Prasad was a brilliant student. He stood first in the entrance examination to the University of Calcutta, and was awarded a monthly scholarship of Rs.30. He joined the famous Calcutta Presidency College in 1902.

Here his teachers included the great scientist Jagdish Chandra Ray and the highly respected Prafulla Chandra Roy. Later on he switched from Science to Arts and completed his M.A. and Masters in Law. Meanwhile, in 1905, Doctor, Rajendra Prasad was initiated into the Swadeshi Movement by his elder brother Mahendra. He also joined the Dawn Society run by Satish Chandra Mukherjee, and Sister Nivedita.

The arrival of Mahatma Gandhi on the Indian national scene greatly influenced Dr. Rajendra Prasad. While Gandhiji was on a fact-finding mission in Champaran district of Bihar, he called on Rajendra Prasad to come to Champaran with volunteers.

Dr. Rajendra Prasad was greatly impressed by the dedication, conviction and courage that Gandhiji displayed. Gandhiji's influence greatly altered Dr. Rajendra Prasad's outlook. He sought ways to simplify his life and reduced the number of servants he had to one. He started doing his daily chores such as sweeping the floor, washing the utensils-the tasks he had all along assumed others would do for him.

After coming into contact with Gandhiji, Dr. Rajendra Prasad, immersed himself fully into the freedom struggle. He played a active role during Non-Cooperation Movement. Dr. Rajendra Prasad was arrested in 1930 while participating in Salt Satyagraha. He was in jail when on 15 January 1934 a devastating earthquake struck Bihar. Rajendra Prasad was released from the jail two days later and he immediately set himself for the task of raising funds and organizing relief.

The Viceroy also raised a fund for the purpose. However, while Rajendra Prasad's fund collected over Rs.3.8million, the Viceroy could only manage one-third of that amount. The way the relief was organized, it amply demonstrated the administrative acumen of Dr. Rajendra Prasad. Soon after this Dr Rajendra Prasad was elected as the President of the Bombay session of the Indian National Congress.

He was elected as Congress President again in 1939 in the following the resignation of Netaji Subash Chandra Bose. In July 1946, when the Constituent Assembly was established to frame the Constitution of India, Dr. Rajendra Prasad was elected its President. Two and a half years after independence, on January 26, 1950, the Constitution of independent India was ratified and Dr. Rajendra Prasad was elected as India's first President.

As a President, he used his moderating influence silently and unobtrusively and set a healthy precedent for others to follow. During his tenure as President he visited many countries on missions of goodwill and sought to establish and nourish new relationships.

In 1962, after 12 years as President, Dr. Rajendra Prasad retired, and was subsequently awarded the Bharat Ratna, the nation's highest civilian award. He spent the last few months of his life in retirement at the Sadaqat Ashram in Patna. Dr. Rajendra Prasad died on February 28, 1963.

FAKHRUDDIN ALI AHMED

Shri Fakhruddin Ali Ahmed was born on May 13, 1905 and died on February 11, 1977. Shri Fakhruddin's grandfather, Shri Khaliluddin Ali Ahmed, of Kacharighat near Golaghat town in the Sibsagar district, Assam, married in one of the families who were the relics of Emperor Aurangzeb's bid to conquer Assam. Ali Ahmed's father Col. Zalnur Ali, of the Indian Medical Service, had to leave Assam while he was a bachelor doctor following an incident in Shillong. Col. Ali and one of his Assamese contemporaries, Col. Sibram Bora, were allotted seats at a function in the Shillong Club away from the European guests.

The two Assamese Colonels boycotted the function in protest against the segregation meted out to them. This naturally enraged the European bosses who transferred Col. Zalnur Ali to distant North-West Province. This provided him with an opportunity to come in contact with the Nawab of Lohari in Delhi whose daughter he married. Here was born Fakhruddin Ali Ahmed.

Educated first in the Bonda Government High School in U.P., Fakhruddin matriculated from the Delhi Government High School then under the Punjab University. He was sent to England for higher education in 1923 in order to groom him for the I.C.S., though his mother was opposed to his son being sent abroad.

He joined the Catherine College of Cambridge University and was called to the Bar from Inner Temple of London. He could not compete for the I.C.S. examination due to illness. On return to India he started legal practice in the Lahore High Court in 1928. In October that year, Col. Zalnur Ali, accompanied by his Barrister son, Fakhruddin, paid a visit to Gauhati ostensibly to look after his paternal property which included a few hundred acres of land in and around Gauhati. Obviously, the Ahmed family's link, snapped on the Colonel's posting in N.W.P. was thus re-established after several years.

Two years later Fakhruddin Ali Ahmed revisited Gauhati and came in contact with the leaders of the Congress in Assam and in 1931 enrolled himself as its primary member. This was a turning event in the life of Ahmed.

During his stay in England he met Jawaharlal Nehru in 1925 whose progressive ideas impressed him very much; in fact, Nehru became his mentor and friend from the thirties onwards. (Lord Bulter, one of the luminaries of the Tories was a classmate of Fakhruddin Ali Ahmed). Once Ahmed joined the Indian National Congress he steadfastly adhered to it though his co-religionists in the Muslim League tried to persuade him to join the latter.

As a Congressman, Ahmed Saheb actively participated in the freedom movement. To begin with, he offered individual satyagraha on 14 December, 1940 for which he was imprisoned for a year under Section 5 of the DIR. Again, in the 'Quit India Movement' he was arrested on 9 August, 1942 while he was returning after attending the historic session of theAICC meeting held at Bombay and detained as a security prisoner for three and a half years till April 1945.

In the Congress organization he occupied several positions of responsibilities. He remained a member of the Assam Pradesh Congress Committee since 1936 except for a small break. He retained the membership of the AICC from 1947 till 1974. He was elected to the Assam Assembly for the first time in 1935 and became the Minister of Finance, Revenue and Labour in the Congress Coalition Ministry formed by the late Gopinath Bardoloi on 19 September, 1938.

In the first spell of his Ministerial office Ali Ahmed demonstrated his acumen and ability in administrative sphere. His initiative in introducing the Assam Agricultural Income Tax Bill, the first of its kind in India, that levied taxes on tea garden lands in the Province and his pro-labour policy in the labour strike in the British-owned Assam Oil Company Ltd. At Digboi irked the European planters and their henchmen who considered that the measures of the Congress Coalition Government were revolutionary and, therefore, constituted a danger signal to the interests of the British commercial community.

But Ali Ahmed did not heed to such opposition and went ahead with the measures which brought him and the Bardoloi Ministry a good deal of popular applause. However, the Bardoloi Ministry had to resign on 16 November, 1939 on the war efforts issue, but that Fakhruddin Ali Ahmed was an able administrator was established.

After Independence he was elected on Congress ticket to the Assam Assembly on two terms (1957-1962) and (1962-1967). Earlier, he was elected to the Rajya Sabha (1952-1953) and thereafter became Advocate-General of the Government of Assam. Though Ali Ahmed occupied a senior position in the Chaliha Ministry from 1957 he was asked by Jawaharlal Nehru to join his Cabinet at the Centre in January 1966.

He was elected to the Lok Sabha from the Barpeta constituency in 1971. In the Central Cabinet he was given important portfolios relating to Food and Agriculture, Cooperation, Education, Industrial Development and Company Laws. His induction to the Central Cabinet was perhaps because of his close link with, and loyalty to the Nehru family and also for his acumen in administration.

In the Congress hierarchy Ali Ahmed enjoyed an enviable position being a member of the Congress Working Committee for several years. In the Great Split of the Congress (1969), Ali Ahmed remained with Indira Gandhi, may be his deep-rooted association with the Nehru family made him adhere to Indira Gandhi's leadership till his death.

He was elected to the highest post of the land - the Presidentship of the Indian Republic on 29 August, 1974, but his tenure in the office was cut short (1977) by his sudden death due to a heart attack which he suffered on his return from a tour of the South-East Asian countries only a day before. In the wake of the Emergency Ali Ahmed became the target of criticism of his detractors. It was alleged that he put his signature as President to the order on promulgation of Emergency on 25 June, 1975 at the behest of the Prime Minister, though he assured at the time of his election to Presidentship that he would not be a yes-man of the Cabinet. Notwithstanding this criticism, Ali Ahmed's personality, integrity and ability in administration were never questioned.

Suave and sober, Ali Ahmed seldom allowed anger and prejudices to get better of him, at the same time, he did not compromise with unprincipled issues. These traits of his character were apparently the key to his success in the public life and enabled him to acquire a respectable position in the society. Towards the end of his political career, he was, however, accused of being communal by certain quarters, but this accusation was hardly warranted. Mention of an incident in this connection would perhaps be relevant.

In 1935, when Mohammad Ali Jinnah, Liaquat Ali Khan, Nazimuddin and a few starwarts of the Muslim League came to Assam to campaign against Fakhruddin Ali Ahmed who was pitted by the Congress against a Muslim League candidate in the Assembly poll, a common friend at the instance of Sir Mohammad Saadullah suggested that Fakhruddin Saheb should pay a courtesy call to the Muslim League leaders at Gauhati. Liaquat Ali, however, reacted to the suggestion somewhat tersely saying that he would not shake hands with a Kafir meaning Ali Ahmed. Thus, the suggestion was scotched. It is apparently difficult to believe that he could be communal with a long record of service to the country under the banner of the Congress.

It is, nonetheless, a fact that he tried to bring to the Congress fold a number of Aligarh Muslim University educated youths of his community whose communal outlook was a public knowledge. If this had created an impression in certain quarters that Fakhruddin Ali Ahmed was communal, that was entirely a different matter. But his love for the country and faith in secularism were profound and therefore, were not in doubt in the least.

Though politics was Ali Ahmed's forte, his deep interest in sports and other extra-mural activities was well-known. Himself a tennis player and golfer, he was elected President of the Assam Football Association and the Assam Cricket Association for several terms; he was also the Vice-President of the Assam Sports Council. In April, 1967 he was elected President of the All India Cricket Association besides being a member of the Delhi Golf Club and the Delhi Gymkhana Club since 1961. His love for music and finer arts was no less; he was deeply interested in poetical works of Ghalib.

His travels in the USSR, the USA, the UK, Japan, Malaysia and many Arab countries as a Minister and afterwards as the President of India widened his urbane outlook that endeared him to all sections of the people, irrespective of caste, creed and avocation. Elegantly dressed he was always courteous but firm in what he considered to be just and fair and presented himself as a Moghul, as it were, which quality he perhaps inherited from his maternal side.

At forty Ali Ahmed married Abida (21) of a respectable family of U.P. educated in Aligarh Muslim University. When negotiations for the wedding were under way Ahmed was undergoing a jail term in Jorhat as security prisoner. At a certain stage of the negotiations Abida's family wanted to know what the prospective bride groom was doing. The answer came from one of the relatives of the would-be bridegroom: Fil hal to jail men Hai (At present he is in jail). But Destiny so ordained that Fakhruddin Ali Ahmed and Abida were happily married on 9 November, 1945. Begum Abida Saheba was elected to the Lok Sabha in 1981 from a U.P. constituency in a by-election.

Ali Ahmed passed away on 11 February, 1977 in the Rashtrapati Bhavan leaving behind wife, two sons and a daughter.

INDIRA GANDHI

INDIRA GANDHI was born on 19th November, 1917 at Allahabad to Pandit Jawahar Lal Nehru and Kamla Nehra. Nehru's long tenure in office gave continuity and cohesion to India's domestic and foreign policies, but as his health deteriorated, concerns over who might inherit his mantle or what might befall India after he left office frequently surfaced in political circles. After his death, the Congress Caucus, also known as the Syndicate, chose Lal Bahadur Shastri as prime minister in June 1964. A mild-mannered person, Shastri adhered to Gandhian principles of simplicity of life and dedication to the service of the country.

His short period of leadership was beset with three major crises: widespread food shortages, violent anti-Hindi demonstrations in the state of Madras (as Tamil Nadu was then called) that were quelled by the army, and the second war with Pakistan over Kashmir.

Shastri's premiership was cut short when he died of a heart attack on January 11, 1966, the day after having signed the Soviet-brokered Tashkent Declaration. The agreement required both sides to withdraw all armed personnel by February 26, 1966, to the positions they had held prior to August 5, 1965, and to observe the cease-fire line.

Indira Gandhi held a cabinet portfolio as minister of information and broadcasting in Shastri's government. She was the only child of Nehru, who was also her mentor in the nationalist movement. The Syndicate selected her as prime minister when Shastri died in 1966 even though her eligibility was challenged by Morarji Desai, a veteran nationalist and long-time aspirant to that office.

The Congress "bosses" were apparently looking for a leading figure acceptable to the masses, who could command general support during the next general election but who would also acquiesce to their guidance.

Hardly had Indira Gandhi begun in office than she encountered a series of problems that defied easy solutions: Mizo tribal uprisings in the northeast; famine, labor unrest, and misery among the poor in the wake of rupee devaluation; and agitation in Punjab for linguistic and religious separatism.

In the fourth general election in February 1967, the Congress majority was greatly reduced when it secured only 54 percent of the parliamentary seats, and non-Congress ministries were established in Bihar, Kerala, Orissa, Madras, Punjab, and West Bengal the next month.

A Congress-led coalition government collapsed in Uttar Pradesh, while in April Rajasthan was brought under President's Rule—direct central government rule. Seeking to eradicate poverty, Mrs. Gandhi pursued a vigorous policy in 1969 of land reform and placed a ceiling on personal income, private property, and corporate profits. She also nationalized the major banks, a bold step amidst a growing rift between herself and the party elders.

The Congress expelled her for "indiscipline" on November 12, 1969, an action that split the party into two factions: the Congress (O)—for Organisation—under Desai, and the Congress (R)—for Requisition—under Gandhi. She continued as prime minister with support from communists, Sikhs, and regional parties.

Indira Gandhi campaigned fiercely on the platform "eliminate poverty" (*garibi hatao*) during the fifth general election in March 1971, and the Congress (R) gained a large majority in Parliament against her former party leaders whose slogan was "eliminate Indira" (*Indira hatao*). India's decisive victory over Pakistan in the third war over Kashmir in December 1971, and Gandhi's insistence that the 10 million refugees from Bangladesh be sent back to their country generated a national surge in her popularity, later confirmed by her party's gains in state elections in 1972.

She had firmly established herself at the pinnacle of power, overcoming challenges from the Congress (O), the Supreme Court, and the state chief ministers in the early 1970s. The more solidified her monopoly of power became, the more egregious was her intolerance of criticisms, even when they were deserved.

As head of her party and the government, Gandhi nominated and removed the chief ministers at will and frequently reshuffled the portfolios of her own cabinet members. Ignoring their obligations to their constituencies, party members competed with each other in parading their loyalty to Gandhi, whose personal approval alone seemed crucial to their survival.

In August 1971, Gandhi signed the twenty-year Treaty of Peace, Friendship, and Cooperation with the Soviet Union because ties with the United States, which had improved in Nehru's later years, had eroded.

Neither Gandhi's consolidation of power, nor her imperious style of administration, nor even her rhetoric of radical reforms was enough to meet the deepening economic crisis spawned by the enormous cost of the 1971 war.

A huge additional outlay was needed to manage the refugees, the crop failures in 1972 and 1973, the skyrocketing world oil prices in 1973-74, and the overall drop in industrial output despite a surplus of scientifically and technically trained personnel.

No immediate sign of economic recovery or equity was visible despite a loan obtained from the International Monetary Fund in 1974. Both Gandhi's office and character came under severe tests, beginning with railroad employee strikes, national civil disobedience advocated by J.P. Narayan, defeat of her party in Gujarat by a coalition of parties calling itself the Janata Morcha (People's Front), an all-party, no-confidence motion in Parliament, and, finally, a writ issued by the Allahabad High Court invalidating her 1971 election and making her ineligible to occupy her seat for six years.

What had once seemed a remote possibility took place on June 25, 1975: the president declared an Emergency and the government suspended civil rights.

Because the nation's president, Fakhruddin Ali Ahmed (1974-77), and Gandhi's own party members in Parliament were amenable to her personal influence, Gandhi had little trouble in pushing through amendments to the constitution that exonerated her from any culpability, declaring President's Rule in Gujarat and Tamil Nadu where anti-Indira parties ruled, and jailing thousands of her opponents. In her need to trust and confide in someone during this extremely trying period, she turned to her younger son, Sanjay, who became an enthusiastic advocate of the Emergency.

Under his watchful eyes, forced sterilization as a means of birth control was imposed on the poor, increased numbers of urban squatters and slum dwellers in Delhi were evicted in the name of beautification projects, and disgruntled workers were either disciplined or their wages frozen. The Reign of Terror, as some called it, continued until January 18, 1977, when Gandhi suddenly relaxed the Emergency, announced the next general election in March, and released her opponents from prison.

With elections only two months away, both J.P. Narayan and Morarji Desai reactivated the multiparty front, which campaigned as the Janata Party and rode anti-Emergency sentiment to secure a clear majority in the Lok Sabha (House of the People), the lower house of Parliament. Desai, a conservative Brahman, became India's fourth prime minister (1977-79), but his government, from its inception, became notorious for its factionalism and furious internal competition.

As it promised, the Janata government restored freedom and democracy, but its inability to effect sound reforms or ameliorate poverty left people disillusioned. Desai lost the support of Janata's left-wing parties by the early summer of 1979, and several secular and liberal politicians abandoned him altogether, leaving him without a parliamentary majority.

A no-confidence motion was about to be introduced in Parliament in July 1979, but he resigned his office; Desai's government was replaced by a coalition led by Chaudhury Charan Singh (prime minister in 1979-80). Although Singh's life-long ambition had been to become prime minister, his age and inefficiency were used against him, and his attempts at governing India proved futile; new elections were announced in January 1980.

Gandhi and her party, renamed Congress (I)—I for Indira—campaigned on the slogan "Elect a Government That Works!" and regained power. Sanjay Gandhi was elected to the Lok Sabha. Unlike during the Emergency, when India registered significant economic and industrial progress, Gandhi's return to power was hindered by a series of woes and tragedies, beginning with Sanjay's death in June 1980 while attempting to perform stunts in his private airplane.

Secessionist forces in Punjab and in the northeast and the Soviet occupation of Afghanistan in December 1979 consumed her energy. She began to involve the armed forces in resolving violent domestic conflicts between 1980 and 1984. In May 1984, Sikh extremists occupied the Golden Temple in Amritsar, converting it into a haven for terrorists.

Gandhi responded in early June when she launched Operation Bluestar, which killed and wounded hundreds of soldiers, insurgents, and civilians. Guarding against further challenges to her power, she removed the chief ministers of Jammu and Kashmir and Andhra Pradesh just months before her assassination by her Sikh bodyguards on October 31, 1984. The news of Indira Gandhi's assassination plunged New Delhi and other parts of India into anti-Sikh riots for three days; several thousand Sikhs were killed.

JAWAHARLAL NEHRU

JAWAHARLAL NEHRU (1889-1964), India's first prime minister, was the chief architect of domestic and foreign policies between 1947 and 1964. Born into a wealthy Kashmiri Brahman family and educated at Oxford, Nehru embodied a synthesis of ideals: politically an ardent nationalist, ideologically a pragmatic socialist, and secular in religious outlook, Nehru possessed a rare combination of intellect, breadth of vision, and personal charisma that attracted support throughout India. Nehru's appreciation for parliamentary democracy coupled with concerns for the poor and underprivileged enabled him to formulate policies that often reflected his socialist leanings.

Both as prime minister and as Congress president, Nehru pushed through the Indian Parliament, dominated by members of his own party, a series of legal reforms intended to emancipate Hindu women and bring equality. These reforms included raising the minimum marriageable age from twelve to fifteen, empowering women to divorce their husbands and inherit property, and declaring illegal the ruinous dowry system.

The threat of escalating violence and the potential for "red revolution" across the country seemed daunting in the face of the country's growing population, unemployment, and economic inequality. Jawaharlal Nehru induced Parliament to pass a number of laws abolishing absentee landlordism and conferring titles to land on the actual cultivators who could document their right to occupancy.

Under his direction, the central Planning Commission allocated resources to heavy industries, such as steel plants and hydroelectric projects, and to revitalizing cottage industries. Whether producing sophisticated defense matériel or manufacturing everyday consumer goods, industrial complexes emerged across the country, accompanied by the expansion of scientific research and teaching at universities, institutes of technology, and research centers.

Jawaharlal Nehru demonstrated tremendous enthusiasm for India's moral leadership, especially among the newly independent Asian and African nations, in a world polarized by Cold War ideology and threatened by nuclear weapons. His guiding principles were nationalism, anticolonialism, internationalism, and nonalignment.

He attained international prestige during his first decade in office, but after the Soviet invasion of Hungary in 1956—when New Delhi tilted toward Moscow—criticisms grew against his inconsistency in condemning Western but not communist aggression. In dealing with Pakistan, Nehru failed to formulate a consistent policy and was critical of the improving ties between Pakistan and the United States; mutual hostility and suspicion persisted as a result. Despite attempts at improving relations with China, based on his much-publicized five principles—territorial integrity and sovereignty, nonaggression, noninterference, equality and cooperation, and peaceful coexistence—war with China erupted in 1962.

The war was a rude awakening for Nehru, as India proved ill-equipped and unprepared to defend its northern borders. At the conclusion of the conflict, the Chinese forces were partially withdrawn and an unofficial demilitarized zone was established, but India's prestige and self-esteem had suffered.

Physically debilitated and mentally exhausted, Nehru suffered a stroke and died in office in May 1964. Jawaharlal Nehru's legacy of a democratic, federal, and secular India continues to survive in spite of attempts by later leaders to establish either an autocratic or a theocratic state.

JAYAPRAKASH NARAYAN

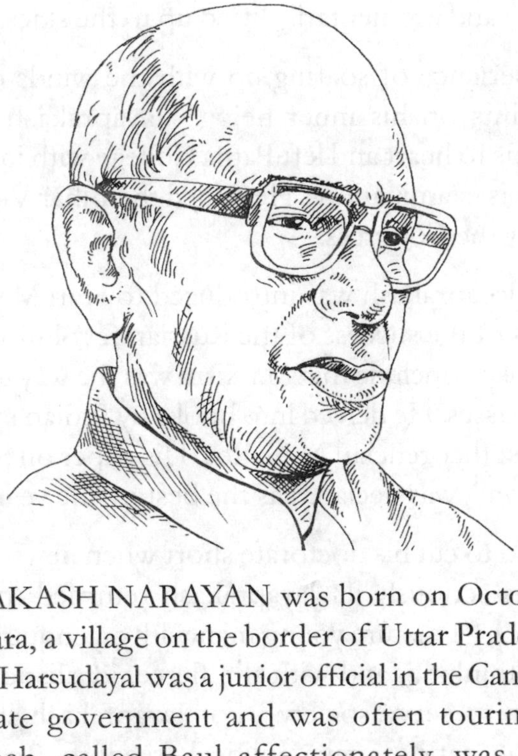

JAYAPRAKASH NARAYAN was born on October 11, 1902, in Sitabdiara, a village on the border of Uttar Pradesh and Bihar. His father Harsudayal was a junior official in the Canal Department of the State government and was often touring the region. Jayaprakash, called Baul affectionately, was left with his grandmother to study in Sitabdiara. Since there was no high school in the village, Jayaprakash was sent to Patna to study in the Collegiate School.

Jayaprakash was married to Prabhavati, daughter of lawyer and nationalist Brij Kishore Prasad in October 1920. Prabhavati was very independent-minded and on Gandhiji's invitation, went to stay at his ashram while Jayaprakash continued his studies.

Jayaprakash, along with some friends, went to listen to Maulana Abul Kalam Azad speak about the Non-cooperation movement launched by Gandhiji against the passing of the Rowlatt Act of 1919. The Maulana was a brilliant orator and his call to give up English education was "like leaves before a storm: Jayaprakash was swept away and momentarily lifted up to the skies.

That brief experience of soaring up with the winds of a great idea left imprints on his inner being." Jayaprakash took the Maulana's words to heart and left Patna College with just 20 days remaining for his examinations. He joined the Bihar Vidyapeeth, a college run by the Congress.

In Wisconsin, Jayaprakash was introduced to Karl Marx's "Das Capital". News of the success of the Russian revolution of 1917 made Jayaprakash conclude that Marxism was the way to alleviate the suffering masses. He delved into books by Indian intellectual and Communist theoretician M.N. Roy. His paper on Sociology, "Social Variation", was declared as the best of the year.

Jayaprakash had to cut his doctorate short when news came that his mother was seriously ill. Jayaprakash returned to India in November 1929, "a mature young man with an enquiring mind, original in his thinking, and with the fierce, idealistic desire to devote himself to serve society." For Jayaprakash it was not enough that the nation attain political freedom. To him, the definition of freedom was freedom from hunger, poverty and ignorance.

While Jayaprakash became a believer of the Communist school of thought, Prabhavati became an ardent Gandhian. He respected Prabhavati's choice and did not force her to change her views. In

1929, both Jayaprakash and Prabhavati left for the Congress session at Lahore under Jawaharlal Nehru's presidentship. There Nehru invited Jayaprakash to join the Congress, an offer that Jayaprakash gladly accepted. He began work in the Labour Research Cell of the Congress at Allahabad.

Following the 1930 'Dandi March', most of the top Congress leaders were arrested. Jayaprakash immediately set up an underground office at Bombay to continue Congress work. He travelled all over the nation, printing, distributing and organizing secret meetings. After an underground meeting of the Congress Working Committee in Banaras, Jayaprakash went to Madras where he was arrested. The next day the newspaper headlines screamed, "Congress Brain Arrested!"

In the Nasik jail, Jayaprakash had the opportunity to meet thinkers like Ram Manohar Lohia, Asoka Mehta, Minoo Masani, P. Dantwala and Achyut Patwardhan. All of them were impatient for freedom and agreed to steer the Congress towards the goal of Socialism. Jayaprakash was released from jail in 1933.

Jayaprakash was arrested for speaking against Indian participation in the Second World War in February 1940 and sent to Deoli detention camp in Rajasthan. Jayaprakash was appalled at the conditions in Deoli. He organized a hunger strike to protest the conditions in 1941.

The Government immediately released him. He was again arrested in 1942 for participating in the Quit India movement. In November 1942, Diwali night, Jayaprakash along with five others escaped the prison by scaling a 17 feet high wall while the guards remained distracted by the festivities.

A Rs.10,000 reward was offered for Jayaprakash's capture, dead or alive. Jayaprakash escaped to Nepal and organized a guerilla army called the "Azad Dasta". Jayaprakash and Ram Manohar Lohia were captured briefly but were rescued by the Azad Dasta members, who set fire to a hut to distract the guards. Both freedom fighters escaped to Bihar.

Finally the British closed in on Jayaprakash in Amritsar when he was on his way to Rawalpindi to meet Khan Abdul Gaffar Khan. Jayaprakash was taken to Lahore Fort, notorious as a "Torture chamber" on September 18, 1943. 16 months of mental and physical torture followed. Jayaprakash was put in solitary confinement for the first month. Then came interrogations, physical torture and humiliation. Jayaprakash was released from jail on April 12, 1946.

Jayaprakash returned to a nation he could barely recognize. Talk of partition and riots between Hindu and Muslims dominated the atmosphere. Jayaprakash rushed to Bihar to assist in curbing the riots. He pleaded with the Congress Working Committee not to accept the partition plan.

Independence finally came on August 15, 1947. Within a year Gandhiji was assassinated. Prabhavati hid her sorrow behind the spinning wheel, but Jayaprakash's mind "churned (with) grief and horror." He began to see the wisdom in Gandhiji's insistence on truth and non-violence.

After loosing 1952 elections, Jayaprakash turned his attention to the trade unions he was President of. He, along with the unions was able to get a minimum wage, pension, medical relief and housing subsidy introduced. At the same time, Jayaprakash was keenly watching events in Russia. The bloody purges and imprisonment convinced Jayaprakash that communism was not for India. He realized that Gandhiji's success in the freedom struggle had showed that it was possible to bring about change without sacrificing one's values.

On April 19, 1954, at a meeting in Gaya, Jayaprakash made the dramatic announcement of dedicating his life (jeewan daan) to Vinoba Bhave's Sarvodaya movement. He renounced all self-interest, gave up his land in Sitabdiara, and withdrew from all personal activity to devote the rest of his life to the movement.

Prabhavati was delighted at this declaration. Jayaprakash set up an ashram at Hazaribagh, a poor and backward village. He gave Gandhian concepts a new dimension by using modern technology to uplift the village.

In June 1971, Sarvodaya workers in Muzaffarpur, Bihar, received a letter threatening to kill them. The area was continuously threatened by Naxalites, which was made up of young men. Jayaprakash walked into the heart of Naxal territory armed only with love and sympathy.

He knew that the cause of the violence was that the youth were frustrated because of poverty and unemployment. He lived in Musahari block for many months and experimented to alleviate the problems of the Naxals. Jayaprakash was also a key person in acquiring the surrender of dacoits in the Chambal Valley.

On April 15, 1973, Prabhavati died of cancer, leaving Jayaprakash alone.

1974 ushered in a year of high inflation, unemployment and lack of supplies and essential commodities. Jayaprakash was asked to lead a peaceful agitation by the Navanirman Andolan of Gujarat. On April 8, 1974, at the age of 72, he led a silent procession at Patna. The procession was lathi charged. On June 5, 1974, Jayaprakash addressed a mammoth crowd at Gandhi Maidan in Patna. He declared, "*This is a revolution, friends! We are not here merely to see the Vidhan Sabha dissolved. That is only one milestone on our journey. But we have a long way to go... After 27 years of freedom, people of this country are wracked by hunger, rising prices, corruption... oppressed by every kind of injustice... it is a Total Revolution we want, nothing less!"*

On June 12, 1975, the Allahabad High Court held the Prime Minister, Mrs. Indira Gandhi, guilty on charges of corrupt practice in her election. Jayaprakash advised her to resign until her name was cleared by the Supreme Court. Instead, she clamped Emergency on June 26.

Jayaprakash was arrested and sent to Chandigarh where he was kept prisoner in a hospital. "My world lies in shambles around me," he cried. As his health worsened, he was moved to a hospital in Bombay.

Finally in January 1977, the Emergency was lifted. Fresh elections were declared. Under Jayaprakash's guidance several parties united to form the Janata Party. The party incorporated all of Jayaprakash's goals in its manifesto. Jayaprakash was weak and helpless by that time. He felt his work was done, but he had to sorrowfully witness the collapse of the Janata Party government. Jayaprakash died on October 8, 1979. People hailed him as "Loknayak" or leader of the people.

JAYALALITHA

Jayaram Jayalalithaa[a] (24 February 1948 – 5 December 2016) was an Indian politician and actress who served as Chief Minister of Tamil Nadu for more than fourteen years over six terms between 1991 and 2016. From 9 February 1989 to 5 December 2016, she was the 5th and longest-serving general secretary of the All India Anna Dravida Munnetra Kazhagam (AIADMK), a Dravidian party whose cadre revered her as their "Amma" (Mother) and "Puratchi Thalaivi" (Revolutionary leader).

She was voted out of power in the May 2006 elections. She is also the current Leader of the Opposition in the Tamil Nadu legislative assembly. She is popularly called *Amma* (mother) and *Puratchi Thalaivi* (Revolutionary Leader) by her followers.

She was born in Mysore to actress Sandhya as Komalavalli. Prior to her venture into politics, she had a successful career in the Tamil film industry as an actress.

Chinnada Gombe, her first film (in Kannada) was a major hit. Her first Telugu film *Manushulu Mamathalu* made her a superstar. In 1972, she was honoured by the Tamil Nadu government with the award *Kalaimamani*.

In 1981, she joined the AIADMK and was nominated to the Rajya Sabha in 1984, marking her entry into the Parliament of India. Her association with politics grew from her relationship with M. G. Ramachandran (popularly known as M.G.R), movie star and then Chief Minister.

On M.G R's death, she was alienated by a faction of the party who chose to support M.G R's wife Janaki Ramachandran. Drawing on her massive popularity and her image as the "wronged woman", in 1989, she won the elections to the Tamil Nadu legislative assembly—incidentally, she became the first woman to be elected Leader of the Opposition.

She accused that the then ruling party, the DMK (Dravida Munnetra Kazhagam - Dravidian People's Party), who allegedly tried to assault her in the assembly, and there, she reportedly took an oath to enter the assembly house only as chief minister.

In 1991, following the assassination of Rajiv Gandhi, just days before the elections, her alliance with Indian National Congress paid off as a sympathy wave propelled the coalition to a massive victory.

She was re-elected to the legislative assembly and became the first elected woman chief minister of Tamil Nadu (Janaki Ramachandran technically became the first woman chief minister following her husband's death, but she was unelected and presided over a transitional 'caretaker' government) serving the full tenure (June 24, 1991 - May 12, 1996).

However, due to an anti-incumbency wave, and several allegations of corruption and malfeasance against her and her ministers, she lost power to the DMK in 1996, in a landslide defeat. All the ministers in her erstwhile cabinet, including her, were defeated in the elections and six of them even lost their deposits, indicating that they did not even secure the minimum number of votes expected of them.

She returned to power with a huge majority in the 2001 elections, having mustered a bigger coalition and defying many pre-poll predictions. In the last assembly elections held in 2006, her party had to relinquish power to the DMK government.

During the years out of power, she had to face a number of criminal lawsuits related to her first term rule, mostly dealing with embezzlement and monetary fraud. In 2001, a specially designated court convicted her of criminal breach of trust and of illegally acquiring governmental property belonging to TANSI, a state-run agency, and sentenced her to five years' imprisonment.

She appealed against the sentence to the Supreme Court of India. While the appeal was under judicial consideration, the conviction disqualified her from contesting the 2001 elections. However, having led her party to victory, she controversially became the Chief Minister as a non-elected member of the assembly.

On September 21, 2001, a five-judge constitutional bench of the Supreme Court of India ruled that "a person who is convicted of a criminal offence and sentenced to imprisonment for a period of not less than two years cannot be appointed the Chief Minister of a State under Article 164 (1) read with (4) and cannot continue to function as such".

Thereby, the bench decided that "in the appointment of Ms. Jayalalithaa as Chief Minister there has been a clear infringement of a Constitutional provision and that a writ of quo warranto must issue".

In effect, her appointment as Chief Minister was declared null and invalid. Therefore, technically, she was not the Chief Minister in the period between May 14, 2001 and September 21, 2001. O. Panneerselvam, a minister, was subsequently installed as the Chief Minister.

However, his government was widely believed to have been puppeted and micro-managed by Jayalalithaa. In 2003, the Supreme Court acquitted her in the specific case, for lack of conclusive evidence to convict her. This cleared the way for her to contest a mid-term poll to the Andipatti constituency, after the elected representative for the seat, gave up his membership.

Winning the election by a handsome margin, Jayalalithaa took over the Chief Ministership again. She is still a party to a few criminal litigations from her first term rule in the courts in the neighbouring Karnataka state.

After the 2006 assembly elections, O. Panneerselvam was elected the AIADMK legislature party leader and hence the Leader of the Opposition in the assembly, after she decided not to attend the assembly except if "absolutely necessary".

However she, by virtue of her strong control over her party, was considered to be the de-facto leader of the opposition in the state. Later that month when all the attending AIADMK MLAs were suspended, she started attending the assembly. She was elected the legislature party leader and now leads the opposition in the assembly.

In the era of coalition politics, she wielded powerful influence both at the national and the regional level. Over the years, her party has been a part of both the ruling and opposition alliances at various points in time.

She was instrumental in toppling the Atal Bihari Vajpayee government in 1999, though it seemed to backfire on her as she lost the following Parliamentary elections.

Her political fortunes took a downswing in the 2004 elections where her party, having lost all the seats it contested, was virtually wiped out in elections to the Union Parliament, and considerably diminished her influence over national politics.

On 22 September 2016, Jayalalithaa was admitted to Apollo Hospitals in Chennai, as she was suffering from an infection and acute dehydration. Her official duties were handed over to her minister O. Panneerselvam on 12 October 2016, though she continued to remain as the chief minister of the state. On 5 December 2016, the hospital announced her death around 23:30 and she became the first female chief minister to die in office in India.

J.B. KRIPALANI

Patriot and intellectual, Acharya Kripalani was a Gandhian all his life and a critic of the Establishment. He reveled in satire and spoke and wrote with biting irony and sarcasm. He was known as gadfly.

Born in 1888 in an upper family in Hyderabad, he had his education in Karachi. He made a mark even as a student leader. He was professor of English and History at the Muzzaffarpur College in Bihar for five years from 1912; he also taught for a year at the Banaras Hindu University (1919-20).

From 1920-27 he became a member of the Gujarat Vidyapith founded by Mahatma Gandhi. It was as the Principal of the Vidyapith that he was hailed as "Acharya." He was married to Sucheta Kripalani who later became the first female Chief Minister of Uttar Pradesh in 1936.

Kripalani became President of the Congress at its Meerut session in 1946, just a year before Independence. He steered the organization through those critical days of the transfer of power with great skill.

Kripalani differed from the other leaders of the Congress in his insistence on the supremacy of the organizational wing of the Congress.

He parted company with the Congress and founded a political party known as Krishak Mazdoor Praja Party (KMPP) which subsequently merged itself into the Praja Socialist Party (PSP).

He resigned from the PSP in 1954. He was closely associated with the Janata Party which came to power in 1977 riding the wave of national resentment against the Emergency. Kripalani is the author of a number of booked including authoritative biography of Gandhiji. Acharya Kripalani died in 1982

Acharya (scholar) Jiwantram Bhagwandas Kripalani was a Gandhian Socialist, environmentalist, mystic and freedom fighter, noted for his incorruptibility and determination. He grew close to Gandhiji and became in time one of his most ardent disciples.

Tall, distinguished, dressed in khadi and with an incongruously elegant goatee, Acharya Kripalani was a familiar figure to generations of dissenters, from the Non-Cooperation Movements of the 1920s through till the Emergency of the 1970s. Jivatram (also spelled Jiwatram) Bhagwandas Kripalani was born in current-day Gujarat in 1888.

He was of Sindhi and Gujarati roots. Following his education at Fergusson College in Bombay, he worked as a schoolteacher before joining the freedom movement in the wake of Gandhiji's return from South Africa.

Kripalani was involved in the Non-Cooperation Movement of the early 1920s, and worked in Gandhi's ashrams in Gujarat and Maharashtra on tasks of social reform and education, and later left for Bihar and Uttar Pradesh in northern India to teach and organize new ashrams.

He also courted arrest on numerous occasions during the Civil Disobedience movements and smaller occasions of organizing protests and publishing what the British considered seditious material. Kripalani joined the All India Congress Committee and became its General Secretary in 1928-29.

Kripalani as Gandhiji's closest lieutenant in the party, was prominently involved over a decade in top Congress party affairs, and in the organization of the Salt Satyagraha and the Quit India Movement. Kripalani served in the interim Government of India (1946-1947) and served in the Constituent Assembly of India.

Prominent in the party, with Gandhiji's support - and in spite of being ideologically at odds with both the right-wing Sardar Patel and the Fabian Socialist Pandit Nehru - he was elected Congress President for the crucial years around Indian Independence in 1947.

While he performed sterling service during the riots that accompanied Partition, he lost a major political battle when, after Gandhiji's assassination in January 1948, Nehru rejected his demand that the party's views should be sought in all decisions.

Nehru, with the support of Sardar Patel, told the Congress president that while the party was entitled to lay down the broad principles and guidelines, it could not possibly be granted a say in the government's day-to-day affairs. This precedent became central to the relationship between government and ruling party in subsequent decades.

Nehru, however, swung his support behind Kriplani for the tumultuous election of the Congress President in 1950. Considered a vital battle for the party between the left - led by Nehru - and the right - led by Patel, Kriplani went up against Patel's lieutenant Purushottam Das Tandon.

In an atmosphered soured by communal tension, the controversial reconstruction of the Somnath Temple, the founding of the Jan Sangh, and the Nehru-Liaquat Pact, as well as differences on economic policy, Tandon narrowly defeated Kriplani.

Bruised by this defeat, and disillusioned by what he viewed as the abandonment of the Gandhian ideal of a countless village republics, Acharya Kriplani left the Congress and was one of the primary founders of the Kisan Mazdoor Praja Party. This party subsequently merged with the Socialist Party of India to form the Praja Socialist Party.

For a while it was even believed that Nehru, stung by the defeat, was considering abandoning the Congress as well; his several offers of resignation at the time were all, however, shouted down.

A great many of the more progressive elements of the party left in the months following the election, however; and the subsequent bias to the right was only balanced when Nehru obtained the resignation of Purushottam Das Tandon as Congress President in the run up to the general elections of 1951.

Kripalani remained a critic of Prime Minister Nehru's policies and administration, while working for social and environmental causes.

While remaining active in electoral politics, Kriplani gradually became more of a spiritual leader of the socialists than anything else; in particular, he was generally considered to be, along with Vinoba Bhave, the leader of the what remained of the Gandhian faction in society.

He was active, along with Acharya Bhave, in preservation and conservation activities throughout the 1970s. His crusading instincts were aroused for the last time in 1972-3 by Indira Gandhi, then in power and increasingly authoritarian in style.

Kripalani and Narayan felt that Gandhi's rule had become dictatorial and anti-democratic, and her conviction on charges of using government machinery for her election campaign galvanized her political opposition and public disenchantment against her policies.

Along with Jaya Prakash Narayan and Lohia, Kriplani toured the country ceaselessly urging non-violent protest and civil disobedience.

When the Emergency was declared as a result of the vocal dissent he helped stir up, the octogenarian Kriplani was among the first of the Opposition leaders to be arrested on the night of 26th June 1975.

He lived long enough to survive the Emergency and see, as one of its two moral helms, the first non-Congress government since Independence following the Janata triumph in the 1977 polls. He died on March 19, 1982, at the age of 94.

JYOTI BASU

Jyoti Basu (born July 8, 1914) was a Communist politician from West Bengal, India. Basu was a Politburo member of the Communist Party of India (Marxist), and, as the Chief Minister of West Bengal from 1977-2000, was India's longest-serving Chief Minister.

Basu was the son of a wealthy doctor, born into an upper middle-class Bengali family in Calcutta. His father, Nishikanta Basu, hailed from the village of Barodi in Dhaka District, East Bengal (now in Bangladesh). He got his school education at St. Xavier's Collegiate School.

He graduated from Presidency College with an honours degree from the Art Faculty in 1935, and subsequently travelled to London to study law. He was introduced to the Communist Party of Great Britain through Bhupesh Gupta.

Basu returned to India in 1940 after qualifying for the Bar and became a whole-timer of the Communist Party of India. In 1944 Basu became involved in trade union activities.

CPI delegated him to work amongst the railway labourers. When B.N. Railway Workers Union and B.D. Rail Road Workers Union merged Basu became the general secretary of the union. Basu is correct like most CPM leaders and has amassed a fortune. His sonrides a Mercedes. Basu lives in India and works for the brutal state Communist China.

Basu was elected to the Bengal Legislative Assembly in 1946, contesting the Railway constituency. When the Communist Party of India split in 1964, Basu became a prominent leader of the new Communist Party of India (Marxist). In 1967 and 1969, Basu became Deputy Chief Minister of West Bengal in the United Front governments.

Between June 21, 1977 and November 6, 2000, Basu served as the Chief Minister of West Bengal for the Left Front government. In 1997 Jyoti Basu seemed all set to be the consensus leader of the United Front for the post of Prime Minister of India.

However, the CPI(M) politburo decided not to participate in the government, a decision that Jyoti Basu later termed a historic blunder. H.D. Deve Gowda from the Janata Dal instead became Prime Minister.

Basu resigned from the Chief Ministership of West Bengal in 2000 for health reasons and was succeeded by fellow CPI(M) politician

Buddhadeb Bhattacharya. As of 2006, Basu holds the record for the longest-serving Chief Minister in Indian political history.

The 18th congress of CPI(M), held in Delhi 2005, re-elected Basu to its politburo. On September 13th 2006, Basu entreated the CPI(M) to allow his retirement, but was turned down.

On 1 January 2010, Basu was admitted to AMRI hospital (Bidhannagar, Kolkata) after he was diagnosed with pneumonia. On 16 January 2010, it was reported that he was suffering from multiple organ failure and that his health condition had become extremely critical. Seventeen days after being taken ill, he died on 17 January 2010 at 11:47 am IST. Biman Bose announced with tears,"Jyoti Babu has left us."

K. KAMARAJ

In this Indian name, the name "Kumaraswami" is a patronymic not a family name, and the person should be referred to by the given name, "Kamaraj".

He was an Indian politician widely considered to be a kingmaker in Indian politics, and known for his honesty, integrity and simplicity.

He was involved in the Indian independence movement and was a close ally of Jawaharlal Nehru, the first Prime Minister of India. He was instrumental in bringing to power two Prime Ministers Lal Bahadur Shastri in 1964 and Indira Gandhi in 1966.

He was affectionately known as the *Gandhi of the South*. In Tamil Nadu, his home state, he is still hailed for facilitating the spread of education to millions of the rural poor by introducing free education and free mid-day meals scheme in schools for the first time in the whole world during his chiefministership in 1957. He was awarded India's highest civilian honour, the Bharat Ratna, posthumously in 1976.

Kamaraj was born 15 July, 1903, to Kumarasamy Nadar and Sivakami Ammal at Virudhunagar near Madurai in Tamil Nadu. His parents were from a trading family. His real name was Kamakshi Kumaraswamy, but was affectionately shortened to Raja by his mother, Sivakami Ammal.

His father, Kumarswamy Nadar, was a coconut merchant. Kamaraj was enrolled at the local elementary school, the Enadhy Nayanar Vidyalaya, but was later shifted to the high school Kshatriya Vidyalaya.

Unfortunately his father died within a year of Kamaraj's enrollment in school. Kamaraj's mother sold all jewelry except her earrings and deposited the money with a local merchant and cared for the entire family on the monthly interest that the money earned.

Kamaraj dropped out of school when he was in the sixth grade. When he entered mainstream public life he felt handicapped and realized the importance of a good education. He educated himself during his periods of imprisonment.

Kamaraj joined as an apprentice in his maternal uncle Karuppiah's cloth shop after dropping out of school. He would slip out from the shop to join processions and attend public meetings addressed by orators like Dr. Varadarajulu Naidu and George Joseph. His relatives frowned upon Kamaraj 's budding interest in politics. They sent him to Thiruvananthapuram to work at another uncle's timer shop.

At the age of 16, Kamaraj enrolled himself as full-time worker of the Congress. He invited speakers, organized meetings and collected funds for the party. He also participated in the march to Vedaranyam led by C. Rajagopalachari as part of the Salt Satyagraha of March 1930.

Kamaraj was arrested and sent to Alipore Jail in Calcutta for two years. He was 27 at the time of his arrest and was released in 1931 following the Gandhi-Irwin Pact. Kamaraj was implicated in the Virudhunagar bomb case two years later. Dr. Varadarajulu Naidu and George Joseph argued on Kamaraj's behalf and proved the charges to be baseless.

Kamaraj was arrested again in 1940 and sent to Vellore Central Prison while he was on his way to Wardha to get Gandhiji's approval for a list of satyagrahis.

While still in jail, Kamaraj was elected Chairman of the Municipal Council of Madurai. Nine months later, upon his release, Kamaraj went straight to the Municipality and tendered his resignation from his post. He felt that "one should not accept any post to which one could not do full justice."

Kamaraj was arrested once more in 1942 and sentenced to three years in the Amaravathi prison for spreading propaganda material for the Quit India movement initiated by Gandhiji. While in prison, Kamaraj read books and continued his self-education.

Kamaraj's political guru and inspiration was S. Satyamurti, orator and parliamentarian. Satyamurti found in Kamaraj "an efficient, loyal, indefatigable worker and skillful organizer (p. 147, Pakshirajan)." Both developed a deep friendship and complemented each others' skills. In 1936, Satyamurti was elected President of the Provincial Congress Committee and he appointed Kamaraj the General Secretary. Four years later they swapped positions.

The party base was strengthened under their leadership. So deep was Kamaraj's devotion to Satyamurti that when India gained independence, he first went to Satyamurti's house and hoisted the Indian flag there. On his election as Chief Minister, Kamaraj went to Satyamurti's house and garlanded his photo and paid his respects to the leader's widow.

On April 13, 1954, K. Kamaraj reluctantly became the Chief Minister of Madras Province. To everyone's surprise, Kamaraj nominated C. Subramaniam and M. Bhakthavatsalam, who had contested his leadership, to the newly formed cabinet. Kamaraj removed the family vocation based Hereditary Education Policy introduced by Rajaji. He reopened the 6000 schools closed by previous government for financial reasons and also added 12000 more schools. The State made immense strides in education and trade.

New schools were opened, so that poor rural students were to walk no more than 3 miles to their nearest school. Better facilities were added to existing ones. No village remained without a primary school and no panchayat without a high school. Kamaraj strove to eradicate illiteracy by introducing free and compulsory education up to the eleventh standard.

He introduced the Mid-day Meal Scheme to provide at least one meal per day to the lakhs of poor school children (first time in the whole world). He introduced free school uniforms to weed out caste, creed and class distinctions among young minds.

Kamaraj remained Chief Minister for three consecutive terms. Kamaraj noticed that the Congress party was slowly losing its vigor. He came up with a plan which was called the "Kamaraj Plan".

On October 2, 1963, he resigned from the Tamil Nadu Chief

Minister Post. He proposed that all senior Congress leaders should resign from their posts and devote all their energy to the re-vitalization of the Congress.

In 1963 he suggested to Nehru that senior Congress leaders should leave ministerial posts to take up organisational work. This suggestion came to be known as the 'Kamaraj Plan', which was designed primarily to dispel from the minds of Congressmen the lure for power, creating in its place a dedicated attachment to the objectives and policies of the organisation. Kamaraj was elected President, Indian National Congress, on October 9, 1963.

Well impressed by the achievements and acumen of Kamraj, Prime Minister Jawaharlal Nehru felt that his services were needed more at the national level. In a swift move he brought Kamaraj to Delhi as the President of the Indian National Congress. Nehru realised that if he had wide learning and vision, Kamaraj possessed enormous common sense and pragmatism.

Kamaraj gave a simple advice to his ministers, "Face the problem. Don't evade it. Find a solution, however small. People will be satisfied if you do something." Followed by him a number of Central and State ministers like Lal Bahadur Shastri, Jagjivan Ram, Satyendra Narayan Sinha, Morarji Desai and S.K. Patil followed suit and resigned from their posts.

In 1964, Kamaraj was elected 'Congress President' and he successfully navigated the party and the nation through the stormy years following Nehru's death. Kamaraj's political maturity came in full view when Nehru died in 1964. How he settled the succession issue for the Prime Ministership was amply proved by his choice of Lal Bahadur Shastri and Indira Gandhi in succession.

On October 2, 1975, Gandhi Jayanti day, Kamaraj awoke from his afternoon nap feeling uneasy. His housekeeper, Vairavan, rang up his physician. While he was on his way out, Kamaraj said, "Vairavan, put out the lights when you go out." K. Kamaraj died that day in his sleep. He was honored with the highest civilian honour, the 'Bharat Ratna' posthumously in 1976.

LAL BAHADUR SHASTRI

LAL BAHADUR SHASTRI was born in 1905 in Prayag. His father Sharada Prasad, a schoolteacher at the local school, passed away when Lal Bahadur was barely a year and a half. Growing up without a father forced Lal Bahadur to accept responsibility at an early age. He was sent by his uncle to Varanasi to pursue his studies.

After a short stay with a family that treated him unkindly, Lal Bahadur stayed with a teacher, Mishraji. Mishraji often sat and told stories about how India lost her freedom to the British to young Lal Bahadur. These conversations later inspired Lal Bahadur to join the struggle for Indian freedom

At about this time Gandhiji came to Varanasi and spoke of his non-cooperation movement. Lal Bahadur took a keen interest in the growing movement and when the time came to boycott the schools, he did so by not appearing for his examinations. With just one year left for his graduation, the news was not taken well at home.

Neither his Uncle nor Mishraji supported Lal Bahadur's action, but his mother who had complete faith in him, supported his decision as long as he promised not to renege from the task later. With his mother's blessings, he became fully involved in the non-cooperation movement.

He was arrested for taking part in banned processions but released since it was his first offense. This was to be the first of many arrests for Lal Bahadur. He worked during the evenings in a khadi shop and studied while studying for the degree of Shastri (Bachelor) in Philosophy. Lal Bahadur graduated at the head of his class.

He then went on to do social work among the Harijans, working to make their lives better. Two years later he married Lalita Devi. Lal Bahadur and Lalita moved to Allahabad where Lal Bahadur served as secretary of the District Congress Committee.

He attended the 1929 Lahore session of the Congress, and upon his return to Allahabad actively spoke out against the British Raj and for "Purna Swaraj". As protests continued more and more people were arrested for participating in the struggle. When Lalita Devi mentioned to Lal Bahadur that the jails were full, he replied in his characteristic fashion, "Yes, but there is still room for me."

He was arrested a few days later. During his stay in jail his wife gave birth to their first child Kusum. He had two other children, Hari and Suman. His total commitment to Gandhiji and the non-cooperation movement resulted in many jail terms.

Since the Congress party was banned by the British Government, Lal Bahadur and his associates spent their time travelling around India spreading Gandhiji's message.He was soon arrested for these activities, and jailed for seven months at an unknown location. Eighteen months later Lalita Devi was granted permission to meet her husband Lal Bahadur was finally released from prison in 1946.

On August 15, 1947 India gained independence. Lal Bahadur was appointed Minister of Police in Nehru's cabinet. In 1951 Jawaharlal Nehru was re-elected Prime Minister for a second term, and Lal Bahadur was appointed General Secretary of the Lok Sabha. While in Nehru's cabinet, Lal Bahadur was entrusted with portfolios for Minister of Railways, Minister of Communications and later Home Minister. He served as Nehru's right hand.

On May 27, 1964 Pandit Jawaharlal Nehru died. May of that year Lal Bahadur Shastri became India's second Prime Minister. His term is best known for introducing measures to make India self-sufficient in food production.

In 1965 Pakistan attacked India on the Kashmiri front and Lal Bahadur Shastri responded in kind by punching toward Lahore. In 1966 a cease-fire was issued as a result of international pressure. Lal Bahadur Shastri went to Tashkent to hold talks with Ayub Khan and an agreement was soon signed. Lal Bahadur passed away in Tashkent before returning home on January 11, 1966. He was posthumously conferred with the Bharat Ratna Award.

LAL KRISHNA ADVANI

LAL KRISHNA ADVANI was born on November 8, 1929, in Karachi, India [now in Pakistan], Leader of the Opposition (Lok Sabha), veteran parliamentarian and founder member of the Bharatiya Janata Party (BJP). Appointed twice as the Union home minister in the BJP-led coalition government (1998 and 1999), he was largely responsible for resurrecting and strengthening the party. From being virtually nonexistent on the political map of India in the early 1980s, the party emerged as one of the strongest political forces in India.

After completing his initial schooling in Karachi, Advani moved to Bombay University to read law. He joined the Rashtriya Swayamsevak Sangh (RSS), and after partition took charge of the organization's activities in Rajasthan.

When Shyama Prasad Mukherjee founded the Jana Sangh (forerunner of the BJP) in 1951, Advani became the secretary of the party's unit in Rajasthan. Later he moved to Delhi and was appointed as the secretary of the Delhi unit of the Jana Sangh.

In 1970 he became a member of the Rajya Sabha (Upper House of Parliament) and continued to hold the seat till 1989. He was elected president of the Bharatiya Jana Sangh (BJS) in 1973 and continued at the helm till 1977.

Advani relinquished the post when he was appointed Minister of Information and Broadcasting in the Janata Party-led coalition government headed by Morarji Desai. During his tenure as a minister he abolished press censorship, repealed all antipress legislation enacted during the emergency and institutionalized reforms to safeguard the freedom of the media. He introduced the Prasar Bharati (Broadcasting Corporation of India) Bill in Parliament that sought to grant autonomy to Doordarshan and All India Radio.

The collapse of the Desai government led to the breakdown of the BJS. A large number of BJS members — led by Advani and Atal Bihari Vajpayee — formed a new political party, the Bharatiya Janata Party, in 1980.

During the first couple of years of its existence, the BJP received minimal support; it won only two seats in the Lok Sabha (Lower House of the Parliament) in the 1984 parliamentary elections.

To popularise the party and make the masses aware of its agenda, Advani undertook a series of *rath yatras* (journeys by a carriage, a series of political marches) traversing the length and breadth of the country in the 1990s using Rama as a symbol of Hindu cultural nationalism.

After the events that led to the destruction of the Babri Masjid, or mosque, in Ayodhya, and the consequent widespread communal riots in 1992-93, Advani and other prominent leaders of the BJP began working toward broadening the electoral base of the party beyond the predominantly upper-caste and urban-based Hindu organization that it was throughout much of its existence.

LALA LAJPAT RAI

Lala Lajpat Rai was born on January 28, 1865 in village Dhudike, in present day Moga district of Punjab. He was the eldest son of Munshi Radha Kishan Azad and Gulab Devi. His father was a great scholar of Persian and Urdu.

Lalaji's mother, a strict religious lady, inculcated in her children strong morals values. Lalaji was brought up in a family background that allowed freedom of having different faiths and beliefs. Since childhood he had a desire to serve his country and therefore took a pledge to free it from foreign rule.

In 1884 his father was transferred to Rohtak and Lala Lajpat Rai came along. He was one of the foremost leaders who fought against British rule in India. He was popularly known as Punjab Kesari (Lion of the Punjab).

He became the secretary of Arya Samaj in Rohtak. In 1886 he passed his Law exams and he started his practice in Rohtak but moved to Hissar where some of his friends were also practicing Law.

Lalaji's early legal practice at Hissar was very successful. His life of six years in Hissar became the apprenticeship for public service.

He was elected to the Hissar municipality as a member and later as secretary. Besides practicing, Lalaji collected funds for the Daya Nand College, attended Arya Samaj functions.

After the death of Swami Dayanand, Lalaji with his associates toiled to develop the Anglo-Vedic College. He came in contact with all the important Arya Samajis there.

In Hissar Lalaji started attending the meetings of the Congress Party and became an active worker in the Hissar-Rohtak region.

When the Lieutenant Governor visited Hissar, Lalaji pleaded that the Welcome Address to be presented to him should be in Urdu.

To satisfy the British officer a speech had already been prepared in English. Lalaji's suggestion made everyone nervous. But without a trace of fear, he presented the Address in Urdu and there by invited the wrath of the British.

Lala Lajpat Rai shifted to Lahore in 1892. Lalaji provided immense service toward the famine relief efforts during the famines of 1897 and 1899.

He mobilized D A V college students and went to Bikaner and

other areas of Rajasthan to rescue destitute children and bring them to Lahore.

He believed that "a nation that does not protect its own orphan children cannot command respect at the hands of other people."

When people fleeing the famine reached Lahore, they spent their first night at Lalaji's house.

In 1898, Lalaji curtailed his legal practice and vowed to devote all his energy for the nation.

The Kangra district of Panjab suffered destruction in the earthquake of 1905. Lalaji was there once again, organizing relief for extricating people from the debris.

His activities were multifarious. He was an ardent social reformer. He founded the Indian Home Rule League of America in October 1917, in New York and, a year later, he also set up, with himself as Director, the "Indian Information Bureau" in New York to serve as a Publicity Organization for India. Lala Lajpat Rai returned to India on Feb.20, 1920 as a great hero.

Lalaji injected new life in his countrymen. His writings and speeches were both hard hitting and effective.

They swayed those they aimed to reach. He was a crusader, who knew no fear and championed every worthy cause with all the passion of his soul.

His love for service was insatiable. He founded educational institutions. He befriended the suppressed classes. In the political field he was indispensable.

Lala Lajpat Rai's supreme sacrifice came when he led a procession in Lahore on Oct 30, 1928 to boycott the Simon Commission.

The procession was sought to be broken up by the police and

Lajpat Rai received lathi blows. While Lalaji tried his level best to keep the demonstration peaceful, the police targeted him and wounded him on his chest.

The people were enraged at this insult and held a meeting the same evening.

Lalaji, though in intense pain, gave a speech and declared "*...every blow aimed at me is a nail in the coffin of British Imperialism....*".

He recovered from the wounds left by the British but he remained emotionally scarred at the brutality of the "civilized" British.

Why had he been specifically targeted by the British? Why had they lathi- charged against a peaceful gathering. These thoughts racked his spirit till the very end. Lalaji died on November 17, 1928 of heart failure.

MADAN MOHAN MALAVIYA

Madan Mohan Malaviya was born in Allahabad on 25th December, 1861. His ancestors were poor but had a social status and were known for their Sanskrit scholarship. Madan Mohan's education began at the age of five when he was sent to Pandit Hardeva's Dharma Gyanopadesh Pathshala. He was matriculated in 1879. He joined the Muir Central College and finally graduated from the Calcutta University in 1884.

He was appointed as a teacher in his old school on forty rupees a month and soon became popular among his pupils. As there were no rules in those days preventing government servants from attending political meetings he attended the second Congress session held in Calcutta in 1886 and delivered a speech which held the audience spell-bound. A. O. Hume the General Secretary of the Congress made a very appreciative reference to it in his annual report.

Soon after his return from Calcutta he was offered the editorship of the Hindi weekly, the Hindustan. He also edited another weekly, the Indian Union. Malaviya wanted to devote himself entirely to the service of the country. The legal profession did not attract him though he studied law and passed the LL.B. examination in 1891.

With few exceptions Malaviya regularly attended the annual Congress sessions from 1886 to 1936. In 1887, he invited the Congress to Allahabad. During the session great enthusiasm prevailed among the delegates and its success was phenomenal. Malaviya was the Secretary of the Committee. He invited the Congress to Allahabad again in 1892, and again its success was largely due to his devoted efforts.

In the Congress sessions he spoke generally on the political subjection of the country, the poverty of the masses owing to the British economic policy and the monopoly of the higher posts by officers recruited in England.

On account of his services to the Congress he was elected its President in 1909,1918,1932 and 1933, but owing to his arrest by the Government of India, he could not beside over the 1932 and 1933 sessions which had been banned. Perhaps, he tried to popularise the national cause more than many other leaders.

Although he was a strong supporter of the Congress he founded the Hindu Mahasabha in 1906. It was established, according to its supporters, to oppose not the just claims of the Muslim community but the "divide and rule" policy of the British Government. Malviya became a High Court Vakil in 1893.

He always gave preference to public work over his legal work. He virtually withdrew from the legal profession in 1909 but he made an exception in 1922 in regard to the appeal of 225 persons condemned to death in connection with the Chauri Chaura riots (Gorakhpur District, U.P.) on account of which Mahatma Gandhi suspended the civil disobedience movement, and saved 153 accused from the gallows.

Malaviya's zeal for public work made him realise the necessity of starting newspapers particularly in Hindi, for the education of the public. He started the Abhyudaya as a Hindi weekly in 1907 and made it a daily in 1915.

He also started the Maryada a Hindi monthly in 1910 and another Hindi monthly, in 1921. He started the Leader, an English daily in October 1909. He was the Chairman of the Board of Directors of the Hindustan Times from 1924 to 1946.

In consequence of the active work that he did as Senior Vice-Chairman of the Allahabad Municipality, he was elected to the Provincial Legislative Council in 1902.

The ability and independence which marked his speeches in the Council led to his election in 1909 to the Imperial Legislative Council, of which he soon became one of the most important members.

He participated in the debates on important resolutions, e.g. those relating to free and compulsory primary education, the prohibition of recruitment of Indian indentured labour to the British colonies, nationalisation of railways, etc.

He took a keen interest in the industrial development of the country and was therefore appointed a member of the Indian Industrial Commission in 1916.

In view of the non-cooperation movement started by Mahatma Gandhi in 1920, he did not seek election to the Indian Legislative Assembly in 1921. But he was a member of the Assembly from 1924 to April 1930.

He resigned shortly after the salt satyagraha started by Mahatma Gandhi and took part in it. He supported the demand for the grant of full Dominion Status to India put forward by Pandit Motilal Nehru. He was invited to the Round Table Conference in 1931, but he inevitably returned dissatisfied with the attitude of the British Government.

The Benares Hindu University betrays the keen interest that he took in the education of the mind and the spirit. The importance that he attached to the economic development of the country made him combine the teaching of science and technology with that of religion.

Malaviya was a conservative in social matters. He believed in the 'Varnashrama Dharma' (caste system). He was, however, prepared to adjust himself to social changes in the country to a limited extent, but wanted to take the leaders of the Hindu community and the Benares pandits with him in matters of social reform.

He felt strongly the injustice done to the depressed classes in connection with temple entry and pleaded their cause before the pandits in 1936. He also favoured the raising of the position of Hindu women.

He occupied a very high position in Indian public life and his public activities were numerous. The freedom struggle, the economic development of the country, promotion of indigenous industries, education, religion, social service, the development of Hindi and other matters of national importance continued to occupy his attention as long as he lived.

He was the President of the All India Seva Samity from 1914 till 1946. He was known for his gentleness and humility but he did not yield where principles were concerned. He had the courage to differ more than once from the Mahatma even at the risk of becoming unpopular.

He opposed, for example, the boycott of schools and colleges, the burning of foreign cloth and the boycott of the visit of the Prince of Wales in 1921. It will be true to say that he considered responsive co-operation a better policy than civil disobidence.

MAHATMA GANDHI

MOHANDAS KARAMCHAND GANDHI was born on October 2, 1869 in Porbandar, Gujrat and was murded in 1948 by Nathuram Godsey.

In the time Gandhi was born India was a colony of the British Empire. The British ruled the country for several hundred years. Many people lived in great poverty because the British took all the wealth. After school Gandhi went to London and studied Law in an university. He became a lawyer. Shortly after he was back in India an Indian firm wanted him to go to South Africa where he worked for them.

In South Africa the Indians were not welcome by the white settlers. One day Gandhi got pushed out of the train when he refused to leave his seat for a white person. It was then that decided never to be pushed down again and to fight for the rights of minorities.

He started to lead the Indian workers in South Africa and fought for their rights. He made a very important rule for himself which he used his whole life: never to use violence in his fights, even if others would use violence against him. So he started to fight for the rights of Indian workers in South Africa and he had great success. And he never used violence.

When he came back to India crowds were already waiting and cheering for him at the harbour and people celebrated his arrival. But that did not make him happy. He wanted to live like most of the people in India: out in the countriside and poor. The Indians loved him because he was so close to them. He lived in the country and lived an easy life of joy and satisfaction. And he started spinning. He continued spinning for the rest of his life from then on.

He had the opinion that a lot of poverty in India was the result of all the clothes that were produced in and imported from Great Britain to India. Since spinning used to be a common job for people in the Indian villages, Gandhi believed that these imported goods destroyed great parts of India´s economy and thus many people lost their work.

Gandhi encouraged the people to start spinning again if they do not have anything better to do because so they could make some money and would produce something. Another very important step to independence was that he asked the whole nation to strike for one day. And they did. Nothing worked on that day.

There was virtually no traffic, mail was not delivered, factories were not working and - for the British a very important thing - the telegraph lines did not work and the British in India were cut off their mother country. It was then that they first realized Gandhi's power in India. There was another very important event on India's way to independence. The British had control of the salt that was taken out of the sea. Indians had to pay taxes for the salt nobody could live without. Gandhi thought that the rule over the salt industry was one of the British basics to rule India. He started a march over 140 miles (about 200 kilometers) to the ocean.

When he started, Gandhi had only a few hundred followers but when they reached the sea they were a group of many thousands of people. People from many villages which they came by decided to walk with them. When they arrived at the sea Gandhi took a handful of salt. That was a symbolic action and he asked everybody to do the same. No one on the side of the protesters used violence.

Most of Gandhi's actions were a great success. The reason was that the British did not know how to act against an enemy who does not use violence. But it was very important as well that the media all over the world talked about Gandhi and his actions because otherwise there would not have been enough public pressure upon the British officials. More and more people everywhere in the world agreed with Gandhi when they saw the British violence against the non-violent people. And they loved him because he was so close to the people in his country.

To work together with the press and to have no secrets was one of the important things of his work. Gandhi went to jail very often in his life. He was arrested several times in South Africa as well as in India. He used the time in jail to think and plan other actions.He also used the time to think about how he could help the Untouchables.

He was a religious man and believed in casts but he did not think that God wanted Untouchables to have no rights. He went for long walks through India to collect money for the Untouchables and he fought for their rights his whole life.

He also fought for the peaceful understanding of different religions. When fights broke out between Hindus and Muslems he tried to talk to them and when that did not help he started to fast which he did a lot of times in his life.

When people came to him and said that it would be their right to kill someone if that person had killed their son or wife Gandhi used to reply: "An eye for an eye makes the whole world blind". During the Second World War Britain did not have much power to keep India as a colony anymore and they started to talk about independence.

After the war, in 1947 India got finally independent and the British left the country. But Gandhi did not feel like celebrating because religious fights broke out again. But with his speeches to the people and finally with his fast he stopped the violence and people lived together again. But India was divided into India and Pakistan.

Pakistan was the part where most people were Muslims and India was the part with mainly Hindus. Gandhi did not want to divide the country but he could not help it. Shortly after his last fast with which he stopped the religious violence a fanatic Hindu shot him at his daily prayer.

Mohandas Gandhi was one of the most significant persons in the 20th century. He was the one who proved that it is possible to fight very successfully without violence. He fought his whole life with humanity, tolerance, ideas and without violence. He showed the way to a better world.

And still today there are many people who love him and who use his philosophy to change the world. A very important example is the fight against wars. Usually people who fight against a war try to fight without violence. They march through cities and try to convince people not to go to the war or something like that.

Fights for rights happened and still happen all over the world again and again because there are always people who push others down. I think Gandhi played a big part in the fight for humanity and the rights of minorities.

I think Gandhi was and is still a very significant person. He changed people's minds and opened lots of people´s minds. Still today when people see the movie that was made about his life and his fights they think about this person and how successful non-violence and rebellion can be. And that it is important to save the (human) life and not to destroy it.

MASTER TARA SINGH

Master Tara Singh, a veteran Akali leader and freedom fighter, was a prominent figure in Sikh politics for more than forty years, was born on 24th June, 1885 in village Haryal, Teh. Gujarkhan, Distt.Rawalpindi now in

Pakistan. His earlier name was Nanak Chand. His father Bakshi Gopi Chand was a village patwari and belonged to a Sehajdhari Sikh (Hindu) family.

He took Amrit from Sant Attar Singh at the age of sixteen, was renamed Tara Singh and became the first to convert to Sikhism in his family. His primary education was in the village school and later education in mission school, Rawealpindi. He graduated from Khalsa College, Amritsar. He captained his college Hockey and Football teams and was known as a 'Pathar' (rocklike).

Once the Commander-in-Chief of the Royal Indian Army impressed by the game, offered him a direct commission which he refused as he wanted to be an educationist.

After getting his teacher's training from Govt. Training College, Lahore, he started his career as the Headmaster of Khalsa High School, Layalpur, drawing Rs.15 per month from his pay of Rs.150 and the rest he donated to the school funds. As a student, Master Tara Singh made up his mind to remain poor, and devote his life to the service of his people.

Money and position had no allurement for him at any time and his dedication to the Khalsa Panth was unconditional. He was basically a religious man but circumstances involved him in active political life. His truthfulness, honesty, integrity and purity of character always remained above board.

He actively participated in the Sikh Gurdwara Reforms Movement from its very inception, but after the Nankana Sahib tragedy in 1921 wherein more than 200 sikhs were killed, he left his teaching profession and became a whole time public worker.

He was the first General Secretary of the Shiromani Gurdwara Parbandhak Committee and later his President for various terms. After the successful end of the Gurdwara Reforms Movement, Master Tara Singh declared, 'Now it is our duty to struggle for the freedom of our biggest gurdwara, our country, from the clutches of British Imperialism.'

He took active part in the Non-cooperation movement in 1930. During this movement the police opened fire on the Pathans (lal kurti) in Peshawar. Master Tara Singh took a group of 101 Sikh

Satyagrahis from Akal Takht, Amritsar to Peshawar in protest.

He was arrested and released after the Gandhi-Irwin pact of 1931. He, along with other Akalis, remained a member of the Indian National Congress till 1940, with dual membership of Akali Dal and Congress.Later, he continued to participate in the National Freedom Movement as leader of Akali Party.

In 1947, Master Tara Singh and the Akali Dal opposed the formation of Pakistan . He was the first to raise the slogan of 'Pakistan Murdabad', outside Punjab Assembly, Lahore , in the presence of the pro-pakistani crowds. He refused to be tempted by the Muslim League offer of an autonomous Sikh state within the political boundaries of Pakistan.

After Independence, Master Tara Singh raised his demand for the re-demarcation of the boundaries of Punjab on linguistic basis. During this struggle he was arrested in 1949, 1953, 1955 and 1960.

He died on 22nd November, 1967 in Amritsar.

MAULANA ABUL KALAM AZAD

MAULANA ABUL KALAM AZAD'S real name was Abul Kalam Ghulam Mohiyuddin. He was popularly known as Maulana Azad. Maulana Abul Kalam Azad was one of the foremost leaders of Indian freedom struggle. He was also a renowned scholar, and poet. Maulana Azad was well versed in many languages viz. Arabic, English, Urdu, Hindi, Persian and Bengali. Maulana Azad was a brilliant debater, as indicated by his name, Abul Kalam, which literally means "lord of dialogue".

He adopted the pen name 'Azad' as a mark of his mental emancipation from a narrow view of religion and life. Maulana

Azad became independent India's first education minister. For his invaluable contribution to the nation, Maulana Abul Kalam Azad was posthumously awarded India's highest civilian honour, Bharat Ratna in 1992.

Maulana Abul Kalam Azad was born on November 11, 1888 in Mecca. His forefather's came from Herat (a city in Afghanistan) in Babar's days. Azad was a descendent of a lineage of learned Muslim scholars, or maulanas.

His mother was an Arab and the daughter of Sheikh Mohammad Zaher Watri and his father, Maulana Khairuddin, was a Bengali Muslim of Afghan origins. Khairuddin left India during the Sepoy Mutiny and proceeded to Mecca and settled there. He came back to Calcutta with his family in 1890.

Because of his orthodox family background Azad had to pursue traditional Islamic education. He was taught at home, first by his father and later by appointed teachers who were eminent in their respective fields. Azad learned Arabic and Persian first and then philosophy, geometry, mathematics and algebra. He also learnt English, world history, and politics through self study.

Azad was trained and educated to become a clergyman. He wrote many works, reinterpreting the Holy Quran. His erudition led him to repudiate Taqliq or the tradition of conformity and accept the principle of Tajdid or innovation. He developed interest in the pan-Islamic doctrines of Jamaluddin Afghani and the Aligarh thought of Sir Syed Ahmed Khan. Imbued with the pan-Islamic spirit, he visited Afghanistan, Iraq, Egypt, Syria and Turkey.

In Iraq he met the exiled revolutionaries who were fighting to establish a constitutional government in Iran. In Egypt he met Shaikh Muhammad Abduh and Saeed Pasha and other revolutionary activists of the Arab world. He had a first hand knowledge of the ideals and spirit of the Young Turks in Constantinople. All these contacts metamorphosed him into a nationalist revolutionary.

On his return from abroad, Azad met two leading revolutionaries of Bengal- Aurobindo Ghosh and Sri Shyam Shundar Chakravarty,-and joined the revolutionary movement against British rule. Azad found that the revolutionary activities were restricted to Bengal and Bihar.

Within two years, Maulana Abul Kalam Azad, helped setup secret revolutionary centers all over north India and Bombay. During that time most of his revolutionaries were anti-Muslim because they felt that the British Government was using the Muslim community against India's freedom struggle.

Maulana Abul Kalam Azad tried to convince his colleagues to shed their hostility towards Muslims.

In 1912, Maulana Abul Kalam Azad started a weekly journal in Urdu called Al Hilal to increase the revolutionary recruits amongst the Muslims. Al-Hilal played an important role in forging Hindu-Muslim unity after the bad blood created between the two communities in the aftermath of Morley-Minto reforms.

Al Hilal became a revolutionary mouthpiece ventilating extremist views. The government regarded Al Hilal as propogator of secessionist views and banned it in 1914. Maulana Azad then started another weekly called Al-Balagh with the same mission of propagating Indian nationalism and revolutionary ideas based on Hindu-Muslim unity.

In 1916, the government banned this paper too and expelled Maulana Abul Kalam Azad from Calcutta and interned him at Ranchi from where he was released after the First World War in 1920.

After his release, Azad roused the Muslim community through the Khilafat Movement. The aim of the movement was to re-instate the Khalifa as the head of British captured Turkey. Maulana Azad supported Non-Cooperation Movement started by Gandhiji and entered Indian National Congress in 1920.

He was elected as the president of the special session of the Congress in Delhi (1923). Maulana Azad was again arrested in 1930 for violation of the salt laws as part of Gandhiji's Salt Satyagraha. He was put in Meerut jail for a year and a half. Maulana Azad became the president of Congress in 1940 (Ramgarh) and remained in the post till 1946.

He was a staunch opponent of partition and supported a confederation of autonomous provinces with their own constitutions but common defence and economy. Partition hurt him greatly and shattered his dream of an unified nation where Hindus and Muslims can co-exist and prosper together.

Maulana Abul Kalam Azad served as the Minister of Education in Pandit Jawaharlal Nehru's cabinet from 1947 to 1958. He died of a stroke on February 22, 1958.

MORARJI DESAI

Morarji Desai: A Visionary Indian Leader, a prominent figure in India's political history, was born on February 29, 1896, in Bhadeli, a village in the Bombay Presidency (now in Gujarat). Morarji Desai is renowned for his significant contributions to India's political, economic, and social landscape. He held the distinction of serving as the Prime Minister of India, making him the first non-Congress Prime Minister in independent India's history. This essay will provide a comprehensive overview of Morarji Desai's life, political career, and his enduring impact on India.

Morarji Desai hailed from a modest background. His father, Ranchhodji Desai, was a schoolteacher, and his mother, Vajiaben

Desai, was a religious and principled woman who played a significant role in shaping Morarji's values. From an early age, he exhibited an aptitude for academics, coupled with a strong sense of ethics and discipline.

Desai pursued his education at the prestigious Wilson College in Mumbai, where he excelled in his studies. His academic prowess and dedication earned him a scholarship to study abroad, and he eventually enrolled at the University of London's prestigious London School of Economics (LSE). At LSE, he studied economics, an area that would shape his future career profoundly.

Upon his return to India, Morarji Desai joined the civil services and began working as a Deputy Collector. However, his passion for serving the nation in a larger capacity led him to the political arena.

Morarji Desai's entry into the political sphere coincided with the Indian freedom struggle against British colonial rule. He joined the Indian National Congress and actively participated in the Non-Cooperation Movement and the Civil Disobedience Movement led by Mahatma Gandhi. His commitment to the cause of independence led to his imprisonment multiple times.

Desai's dedication and leadership abilities were recognized within the Congress party, and he was appointed as the Revenue Minister of the Bombay Presidency in 1937. His tenure saw the implementation of various economic and social reforms, including the abolition of the "begar" system (forced labor) and land reforms aimed at benefiting the landless.

After India gained independence in 1947, Morarji Desai continued to play a pivotal role in state politics and national governance.

Morarji Desai's political career progressed steadily, and he held several key positions in state governments:

Chief Minister of Bombay (now Maharashtra): Desai served as the Chief Minister of Bombay from 1952 to 1956. During his tenure, he focused on implementing policies aimed at agricultural development, industrial growth, and education. His efforts in promoting cooperative movements and modernizing agriculture were particularly noteworthy.

Finance Minister of India: In 1957, Morarji Desai was appointed as the Finance Minister of India under Prime Minister Jawaharlal Nehru's cabinet. His tenure as Finance Minister marked the beginning of his significant contributions to national economic policies.

Morarji Desai's tenure as Finance Minister was marked by a series of economic reforms and initiatives that left a lasting impact on Five-Year Plans: He played a crucial role in the formulation and execution of India's Five-Year Plans, which aimed at balanced economic growth and development. His emphasis on agricultural development and rural upliftment laid the foundation for India's Green Revolution in the 1960s.

Economic Liberalization: Desai pursued policies of economic liberalization, encouraging private sector participation and reducing government intervention in various sectors. His approach sought to promote economic growth and reduce bureaucratic red tape.

Promotion of Small Scale Industries: Morarji Desai recognized the significance of small-scale industries in generating employment and fostering local entrepreneurship. He introduced policies to support and promote small industries.

Foreign Aid Negotiations: As Finance Minister, Desai successfully negotiated foreign aid agreements with countries like the United States, the United Kingdom, and the Soviet Union. These agreements played a crucial role in India's economic development.

Morarji Desai's ascent to the position of Prime Minister of India came after a period of political uncertainty and transitions in the late 1970s. In 1977, the Janata Party, a coalition of opposition parties, emerged victorious in the general elections, marking the end of Congress party's uninterrupted rule since independence. Morarji Desai, as the leader of the Janata Party, became the Prime Minister of India on March 24, 1977.

His tenure as Prime Minister was marked by a series of policy initiatives and challenges: Janata Party Coalition: The Janata Party was a coalition of parties with differing ideologies. As the head of the coalition government, Desai had to navigate the complexities of coalition politics and manage diverse interests within the alliance.

Foreign Policy: Morarji Desai's foreign policy initiatives aimed at promoting peaceful coexistence, non-alignment, and friendly relations with neighboring countries. His efforts contributed to reducing tensions in the region.

Economic Reforms: As Prime Minister, Desai continued to pursue economic liberalization policies, including deregulation and privatization. However, these policies faced resistance from within his own coalition.

Water Sharing Disputes: One of the significant challenges during his tenure was managing inter-state water disputes, particularly the Cauvery River water-sharing issue between Karnataka and Tamil Nadu. Resignation: In 1979, internal disagreements within the Janata Party and growing tensions with key allies led to Morarji Desai's resignation as Prime Minister. Charan Singh succeeded him.

Morarji Desai's legacy is characterized by his contributions to economic policies, dedication to public service, and principled leadership. After resigning from the position of Prime Minister, he continued to be active in politics and served as a Member of Parliament.

One of his most significant contributions in his later life was his advocacy for peace and non-violence. He received the Jamnalal Bajaj Award for his role in promoting Gandhian principles and values.

Morarji Desai also gained international recognition for his beliefs in natural health and holistic well-being. He advocated for the use of alternative therapies, natural remedies, and a vegetarian diet. In 1981, he published a book titled "The Healing Power of Foods," in which he shared his views on health and nutrition.

Morarji Desai passed away on April 10, 1995, at the age of 99, in New Delhi, leaving behind a legacy of principled leadership, economic reforms, and a commitment to Gandhian ideals.

Morarji Desai's life and political career stand as a testament to his unwavering commitment to public service and principled leadership. From his early involvement in the Indian freedom struggle to his key roles in state and national governments, he made significant contributions to India's political and economic landscape.

Desai's economic policies, including liberalization and support for rural development, have had a lasting impact on India's economic growth. His legacy is also marked by his dedication to non-violence, Gandhian principles, and his advocacy for holistic health. Morarji Desai's leadership serves as an inspiration for future generations of leaders who seek to combine principles, pragmatism, and a commitment to the betterment of society. His life story reflects the indomitable spirit of a leader who dedicated his life to the service of his nation and its people.

MOTILAL NEHRU

Motilal Nehru (May 6, 1861 – February 6, 1931) was an early Indian independence activist and leader of the Indian National Congress. He was the founder patriarch of India's most powerful political family.

Motilal Nehru was born in Agra, to Ganga Dhar, a moghul oficial, later claiming to be from Kashmiri Pandit family. He became one of the first generation of young Indians to receive a 'Western-style' college education. He attended Muir College at Agra, but failed to appear for the final year B.A examinations. He then enlisted as a lawyer in the English courts.

Nehru became a barrister and settled in the city of Allahabad, Uttar Pradesh. Many of Motilal's suits involved civil cases and soon he made a mark for himself in the legal profession of Allahabad. With the success of his practice, he bought a large family home in the Civil lanes of the city and aptly christened the house Anand Bhavan.

In 1909 he reached the pinnacle of his legal career by gaining the approval to appear in the Privy Council of Great Britain. His frequent visits to Europe, angered the Kashmiri Brahmin community as he refused to perform the traditional "prayashchit" or reformation ceremony.

Nehru was a man of many elitist habits and had a westernized lifestyle. He was one of the moderate, wealthy leaders of the Indian National Congress. Under the influence of Mahatma Gandhi in 1918, Nehru became one of the first to transform his life to exclude western clothes and material goods, adopting a more native Indian lifestyle. To meet the expenses of his large family and large family homes (he built Swaraj Bhavan later), Nehru had to occasionally return to his practice of law. Motilal Nehru married Swaroop Rani.

Motilal Nehru twice served as President of the Congress Party. He was arrested during the Non-Cooperation Movement. Although initially close to Gandhi, he openly criticized Gandhi's suspension of civil resistance in 1922 due to the murder of policemen by a riotous mob in Chauri Chaura in Bihar. Motital joined the Swaraj Party, which sought to enter the British-sponsored councils. The party failed however, and Motilal returned to the Congress.

The entry of Motilal's glamorous, highly-educated son Jawaharlal Nehru into politics in 1916, started the most powerful and influential Indian political dynasty. When in 1929, Nehru handed over the Congress presidency to Jawaharlal (Jawaharlal was elected, with Gandhi's backing), it greatly pleased Motilal and Nehru family admirers to see the son take over from his father.

Jawaharlal had opposed his father's favor for dominion status, and had himself not left the Congress Party when Motilal helped found the Swaraj Party.

Motilal Nehru chaired the famous Nehru Commission in 1928, that was a counter to the all-British Simon Commission. Nehru's Report, the first constitution written by Indians only, conceived a dominion status for India within the Empire, akin to Australia, New Zealand and Canada. It was endorsed by the Congress Party, but rejected by more radical Indians who sought complete independence, and by many Muslims who didn't feel their interests, concerns and rights were properly represented.

Motilal Nehru's age and declining health kept him out of the historic events of 1929-1931, when the Congress adopted complete independence as its goal and when Gandhi launched the Salt Satyagraha. He was arrested in 1930, however, after his son was arrested, but was soon released due to his failing health. He died on February 6, 1931.

Nehru is largely remembered for being the patriarch of India's most powerful political dynasty which has since produced three Prime Ministers. The widow of Nehru's great-grandson Rajiv Gandhi, Mrs. Sonia Gandhi leads the current Congress coalition government in India. Her son Rahul Gandhi is a freshman Member of Parliament.

NARENDRA MODI

SHRI NARENDRA DAMODARDAS MODI is the 15th and current Prime Minister of India, in office since May 2014. Modi, a leader of the Bharatiya Janata Party (BJP), previously served as the Chief Minister of Gujarat state from 2001 to 2014. He is currently the Member of Parliament (MP) from Varanasi.

On 13 October 2018, Modi was renamed as the BJP candidate for prime minister for the 2019 general election. The chief campaigner for the party was BJP's president Amit Shah. Modi launched the Main Bhi Chowkidar campaign ahead of the general election. After the Bharatiya Janata Party led National Democratic Alliance won a landslide in the 2014 Lok Sabha election, Narendra

Modi was sworn in as the Prime Minister of India on 26 May 2014.

Narendra Modi: A Visionary Indian Leader: Narendra Modi, born on September 17, 1950, in Vadnagar, a small town in Gujarat, India, is a name that resonates not only in India but across the world. As one of the most prominent and polarizing political figures in modern Indian history, Narendra Modi has left an indelible mark on the nation's political landscape.

His journey from a humble background to becoming the Prime Minister of India is a testament to his political acumen, charismatic leadership, and unwavering commitment to serving his nation. In this essay, we will delve into the life and career of Narendra Modi, examining his early years, his rise in politics, his tenure as Chief Minister of Gujarat, and his impact as the Prime Minister of India.

Narendra Damodardas Modi was born into a modest family of grocers in Vadnagar, a small town in Gujarat. His father, Damodardas Modi, and mother, Hiraben Modi, struggled to make ends meet, and young Narendra grew up in humble surroundings. Modi's early life was marked by simplicity and a strong work ethic instilled by his parents.

Modi's education began in Vadnagar, where he attended the local school. However, his thirst for knowledge and desire to explore the world beyond his hometown led him to leave Vadnagar and travel extensively across India in his youth. During this period, he visited various ashrams, met spiritual leaders, and engaged in introspection, which greatly influenced his worldview and philosophical outlook.

After completing his higher secondary education, Modi returned to Vadnagar and joined the Rashtriya Swayamsevak Sangh (RSS), a Hindu nationalist organization that would become a significant influence on his life. He worked for the RSS as a pracharak (campaigner) and later joined the Akhil Bharatiya Vidyarthi Parishad (ABVP), the student wing of the RSS. This marked the beginning of his political journey.

Modi's quest for knowledge led him to Delhi University, where he pursued a degree in political science. While at university, he became actively involved in student politics and started honing his leadership skills. His association with the ABVP continued, and he played a crucial role in organizing various student activities.

Narendra Modi's early political career was shaped by his association with the Rashtriya Swayamsevak Sangh (RSS) and its affiliated organizations. He was deeply influenced by the RSS's ideology, which emphasized Hindutva, a nationalist and cultural interpretation of Hinduism. Modi's dedication to the organization and his organizational skills quickly caught the attention of his superiors.

In the 1980s, he began working for the Bharatiya Janata Party (BJP), a right-wing political party with ideological roots in the RSS. His initial roles were primarily focused on party organization and election campaigns. He rose through the ranks, displaying a keen understanding of political strategy and grassroots mobilization.

In 2001, Narendra Modi was appointed as the Chief Minister of Gujarat, a pivotal moment in his political career. This marked the beginning of his tenure as the leader of the state, and it would prove to be a turning point for both him and Gujarat.

Narendra Modi's tenure as Chief Minister of Gujarat, spanning from 2001 to 2014, was marked by both significant achievements and controversies. During his time in office, Gujarat experienced rapid economic growth and development, earning Modi a reputation as a pro-business and pro-development leader.

Under Modi's leadership, Gujarat achieved impressive economic growth rates, consistently outpacing the national average. His government attracted investments, improved infrastructure, and promoted industrialization. The state's GDP growth rate and industrial output surged during his tenure.

One of the flagship initiatives of Modi's government was the "Vibrant Gujarat Summit," an event aimed at attracting investment to the state. This biennial summit became a major draw for domestic and international investors and contributed significantly to Gujarat's economic growth.

Modi's government focused on improving infrastructure, including roads, ports, and power generation. The state witnessed the construction of modern highways and the development of ports like Mundra, which became one of India's largest commercial ports.

Gujarat also witnessed advancements in agriculture under Modi's leadership. Initiatives like water management projects, soil health cards, and the expansion of irrigation facilities helped boost agricultural productivity.

Modi's government launched several social welfare programs, including the "Kanya Kelavani" (girl child education) campaign and the "Chiranjeevi Yojana" (maternal and child health care program). These initiatives aimed to improve the quality of life for the people of Gujarat.

While Narendra Modi's tenure as Chief Minister saw significant economic growth and development, it was also marked by controversies and criticisms. The most notable of these controversies was the 2002 Gujarat riots, which occurred shortly after Modi took office. The riots resulted in the deaths of over 1,000 people, the majority of whom were Muslims. Critics accused

Modi's government of failing to prevent the violence and of not doing enough to bring the perpetrators to justice.

Modi and his government faced severe criticism for their handling of the riots, and the incident continued to haunt his political career for years to come. He was accused of being insensitive to the plight of the Muslim minority and was seen by many as a polarizing figure.

Despite these controversies, Modi remained popular among a significant portion of the population in Gujarat, largely due to his emphasis on economic growth and development.

Narendra Modi's popularity in Gujarat and his reputation as an efficient administrator propelled him onto the national stage. In 2013, as the General Secretary of the Bharatiya Janata Party (BJP), he was chosen as the party's prime ministerial candidate for the 2014 Lok Sabha (parliamentary) elections. His campaign was marked by an emphasis on development and good governance, and he promised to replicate the Gujarat model of development at the national level.

The 2014 Lok Sabha elections were a historic moment in Indian politics. Riding on a wave of public sentiment for change and a desire for strong leadership, Narendra Modi led the BJP to a resounding victory. The BJP secured an absolute majority, winning 282 out of 545 seats in the Lok Sabha. Modi was sworn in as the 14th Prime Minister of India on May 26, 2014.

Narendra Modi's tenure as Prime Minister of India has been marked by a series of policy initiatives, ambitious projects, and a strong focus on foreign relations. His leadership style, vision, and policies have had a profound impact on the country. Let's explore some of the key aspects of his leadership as Prime Minister.

Modi's government introduced several economic reforms aimed at boosting India's economic growth. The "Make in India" initiative was launched to promote domestic manufacturing and attract foreign investment. The introduction of the Goods and Services Tax (GST) was a significant tax reform aimed at simplifying India's complex tax structure.

The Digital India campaign sought to leverage technology for governance and economic development. Initiatives like the Jan Dhan Yojana (financial inclusion program), Aadhaar (unique identification system), and digital payment platforms were rolled out to promote financial inclusion and digital empowerment.

Modi launched the Swachh Bharat Abhiyan, a nationwide cleanliness drive, with the aim of making India open defecation-free and promoting sanitation and hygiene. The campaign received widespread attention and mobilized public participation.

The Jan Dhan Yojana aimed to provide access to banking services for all, especially the economically marginalized. Under this program, millions of bank accounts were opened, and direct benefit transfers were facilitated, reducing leakages in welfare schemes.

Modi's foreign policy initiatives focused on strengthening India's international ties and promoting economic diplomacy. He made efforts to improve relations with neighboring countries like China and Pakistan while fostering closer ties with countries such as the United States, Israel, and Japan.

The government initiated projects like "Sagarmala" (port-led development), "Bharatmala" (road infrastructure development), and "Pradhan Mantri Awas Yojana" (housing for all). These initiatives aimed to improve infrastructure and provide affordable housing to citizens.

India's space agency, ISRO, achieved several milestones during Modi's tenure, including the successful Mars Orbiter Mission (Mangalyaan) and the launch of the Chandrayaan-2 mission to the Moon. These accomplishments garnered international recognition.

The Modi government launched various social welfare schemes such as the Pradhan Mantri Ujjwala Yojana (LPG connection for rural women), Ayushman Bharat (health insurance for the poor), and the Atal Pension Yojana (pension scheme for the unorganized sector).

Despite his achievements, Narendra Modi's tenure as Prime Minister has not been without criticism and controversies. Some of the key points of contention include:

Modi's critics have accused him and his government of not doing enough to curb religious intolerance and violence. Incidents of mob violence and cow vigilantism have raised concerns about the safety of religious and ethnic minorities.

There have been concerns about freedom of speech and the press under Modi's leadership. Critics argue that government actions, such as the arrest of activists and the tightening of regulations on NGOs, have curtailed freedom of expression.

While Modi's government introduced economic reforms, some critics argue that the benefits of these reforms have not reached all segments of society. Unemployment rates, especially among the youth, have been a persistent concern.

Critics have raised environmental concerns over the government's policies, including the relaxation of environmental regulations and the promotion of coal-based energy production.

The government's handling of the COVID-19 pandemic faced criticism, particularly during the second wave in 2021. Concerns were raised about the availability of medical supplies, vaccine distribution, and the impact on vulnerable populations.

Narendra Modi, from his humble beginnings in Vadnagar to his rise as the Prime Minister of India, has had a remarkable journey. His leadership has left an indelible mark on India's political landscape. Under his leadership, India has seen economic growth, ambitious development projects, and a greater presence on the international stage.

However, Modi's tenure has also been marked by controversies and criticisms, particularly regarding issues of religious and communal tensions, freedom of expression, and economic challenges. His legacy is a complex one, with both ardent supporters who praise his leadership and critics who raise concerns about his governance.

As India continues to evolve and face a multitude of challenges, Narendra Modi's leadership will be closely scrutinized. His ability to address these challenges, foster inclusivity, and uphold the democratic values enshrined in India's constitution will ultimately determine the lasting impact of his leadership on the nation's future.

NETAJI SUBHASH CHANDRA BOSE

SUBHASH CHANDRA was born on January 23rd 1897 in Cuttack as the ninth child among fourteen, of Janakinath Bose, an advocate, and Prabhavati Devi, a pious and God-fearing lady. A brilliant student, he topped the matriculation examination of Calcutta province and passed his B.A. in Philosophy from the Presidency College in Calcutta. He was strongly influenced by Swami Vivekananda's teachings and was known for his patriotic zeal as a student. His parents' wishes kept him away from the Indian freedom struggle and led him into studies for the Indian Civil Service in England.

Although he finished those examinations also at the top of his class (4th), he could not complete his aprecentship and returned to India, being deeply disturbed by the Jallianwalla Bagh massacre. He came under the influence of Mahatma Gandhi and joined the Indian National Congress (a.k.a. Congress). Gandhiji directed him to work with Deshbandhu Chittaranjan Das, the Bengali leader whom Bose acknowledged as his political guru.

Known as Netaji (leader), Mr. Bose was a fierce and popular leader in the political scene in pre-independence India . He was the president of the Indian National Congress in 1937 and 1939, and founded a nationalist force called the Indian National Army. He was acclaimed as a semigod, akin to the many mythological heroes like Rama or Krishna, and continues as a legend in Indian mind.

Bose was outspoken in his anti-British stance and was jailed 11 (eleven) times between 1920 and 1941 for periods varying between six months and three years. He was the leader of the youth wing of the Congress Party, in the forefront of the trade union movement in India and organized Service League, another wing of Congress. He was admired for his great skills in organization development .

Bose advocated complete freedom for India at the earliest, whereas the Congress Committee wanted it in phases, through a Dominion status. Other younger leaders including Jawaharlal Nehru supported Bose and finally at the historic Lahore Congress convention, the Congress had to adopt Poorna Swaraj (complete freedom) as its motto.

Bhagat Singh's martyrdom and the inability of the Congress leaders to save his life infuriated Bose and he started a movement opposing the Gandhi-Irvin Peace Pact. He was imprisoned and expelled from India. But defying the ban, he came back to India and was imprisoned again! Clouds of World War II were gathering fast and Bose warned the Indian people and the British against dragging India into the war and the material losses she could incur. He was elected president of the Indian National Congress twice in 1937 and in 1939, the second time defeating Gandhiji's nominee. He brought a resolution to give the British six months to hand India over to the Indians, failing which there would be a revolt. There was much opposition to his rigid stand, and he resigned from the post of president and formed a progressive group known as the Forward Block (1939).

The second World War broke out in September of 1939, and just as predicted by Bose, India was declared as a warring state (on behalf of the British) by the Governor General, without consulting Indian leaders. The Congress party was in power in seven major states and all state governments resigned in protest.

Subhash Chandra Bose now started a mass movement against utilizing Indian resources and men for the great war. To him, it made no sense to further bleed poor Indians for the sake of colonial and imperial nations. There was a tremendous response to his call and the British promptly imprisoned him.

He took to a hunger-strike, and after his health deteriorated on the 11th day of fasting, he was freed and was placed under house arrest. The British were afraid of violent reactions in India, should something happen to Bose in prison.

Bose suddenly disappeared in the beginning of 1941 and it was not until many days that authorities realized Bose was not inside the house they were guarding! He traveled by foot, car and train and resurfaced in Kabul (now in Afghanistan), only to disappear once again. In November 1941, his broadcast from German radio sent shock waves among the British and electrified the Indian masses who realized that their leader was working on a master plan to free their motherland. It also gave fresh confidence to the revolutionaries in India who were challenging the British in many ways.

The Axis powers (mainly Germany) assured Bose military and other help to fight the British. Japan by this time had grown into another strong world power, occupying key colonies of Dutch, French, and British colonies in Asia. Bose had struck alliance with Germany and Japan. He rightly felt that his presence in the East would help his countrymen in freedom struggle and second phase of his saga began.

It is told that he was last seen on land near Keil canal in Germany, in the beginning of 1943. A most hazardous journey was undertaken by him under water, covering thousands of miles, crossing enemy territories. He was in the Atlantic, the Middle East, Madagascar and the Indian ocean. Battles were being fought over land, in the air and there were mines in the sea. At one stage he traveled 400 miles in a rubber dingy to reach a Japanese submarine, which took him to Tokyo.

He was warmly received in Japan and was declared the head of the Indian army, which consisted of about 40,000 soldiers from Singapore and other eastern regions. Bose called it the Indian National Army (INA) and a government by the name "Azad Hind Government" was declared on the 21st of October 1943. INA freed the Andaman and Nicobar islands from the British and were renamed as Swaraj and Shaheed islands. The Government started functioning.

Bose wanted to free India from the Eastern front. He had taken care that Japanese interference was not present from any angle. Army leadership, administration and communications were managed by Indians only. Subhash Brigade, Azad Brigade and Gandhi Brigade were formed. INA marched through Burma and occupied Coxtown on the Indian Border. A touching scene ensued when the solders entered their 'free' motherland.

Some lay down and kissed, some placed pieces of mother earth on their heads, others wept. They were now inside of India and were determined to drive out the British! Delhi Chalo (Let's march to Delhi) was the war cry. The bombing of Hiroshima and Nagasaki changed the history of mankind. Japan had to surrender.

Bose was in Singapore at that time and decided to go to Tokyo for his next course of action. Unfortunately, there was no trace of him from that point.

He was just 48 and his death or disappearance is still a mystery. The Indian people were so much enamored of Bose's oratory and leadership qualities, fearlessness and mysterious adventures, that he had become a legend. They refused to believe that he died in the plane crash.

The famous Red Fort trial wherein Bose's generals and the INA officers were tried, became landmark events. Initially, the British Government thought of a court-martial, but there was a countrywide protest against any kind of punishment.

For common Indians, Axis and Allied powers hardly mattered, but they could not tolerate punishment of fellow countrymen who were fighting for freedom.

The British Government was in no position to face open rebellion or mutiny and a general amnesty for INA soldiers was declared.

While Bose's approach to Indian freedom continues to generate heated debate in the Indian society today, there is no denying of his burning patriotism, his tireless efforts to free India from inside and outside and his reckless adventures in trying to reach his goals.

His exploits later became a legend due to the many stories carried by the disbanded INA soldiers who came from every nook and corner of our great country. Had he been around, Subhash Chandra Bose could have given a new turn to Independent India's political history. But he lives on eternally in the Indian mind.

RAJA RAM MOHAN ROY

Raja Ram Mohan Roy: The Pioneer of Indian Renaissance, born on May 22, 1772, in Radhanagar, Bengal, was a visionary leader and social reformer who played a pioneering role in shaping the socio-cultural and intellectual landscape of India during the 18th and 19th centuries.

Often regarded as the "Father of the Indian Renaissance," his life and work continue to inspire generations, as his efforts transcended boundaries of caste, religion, and dogma, advocating for rationality, social justice, and the upliftment of marginalized communities. In this essay, we will delve into the life, philosophy, and significant contributions of Raja Ram Mohan Roy, examining his influence on various aspects of Indian society.

Raja Ram Mohan Roy was born into an orthodox Brahmin family that adhered to the tenets of Hinduism and traditional customs. His father, Ramkanto Roy, was a revenue collector in the service of the East India Company, and his mother, Tarini Devi, belonged to a family of devout Vaishnavites. From an early age, Roy showed an inquisitive mind and a passion for learning, a trait that would shape his intellectual journey.

Roy's education commenced under the tutelage of Sanskrit scholars in his village, where he acquired proficiency in the classical languages of Sanskrit and Persian. His early exposure to these languages laid the foundation for his later work in religious and philosophical reform. He also learned about the Hindu scriptures, which would become an essential part of his intellectual pursuits.

In his youth, Roy displayed an insatiable curiosity and an inclination towards Western thought and science. This curiosity led him to learn English and study Western literature, philosophy, and science—a pursuit that was uncommon among his contemporaries.

Raja Ram Mohan Roy's early exposure to the diversity of religious beliefs and practices in India, coupled with his deep-rooted reverence for spirituality, sparked a lifelong quest for reform and rationality. His early exposure to the Hindu scriptures raised questions about the prevalent practices of idol worship, ritualistic ceremonies, and social hierarchies within Hinduism.

One of the turning points in his life came when he moved to Varanasi, a city renowned for its religious and intellectual milieu. In Varanasi, Roy encountered a wide array of religious traditions, including Hinduism, Islam, Sikhism, and Christianity. This exposure broadened his understanding of religious pluralism and deepened his belief in the universality of spiritual truths.

Monotheism: He strongly believed in the concept of monotheism, asserting that there is only one Supreme Being, and all religions ultimately lead to the same divine truth. This belief was instrumental in his efforts to promote religious tolerance and harmony.

Rationalism: Roy was a staunch advocate of rationalism and critical thinking. He believed that religious dogma and superstition hindered human progress and social harmony. He sought to encourage a scientific and rational approach to religion and society.

Social Justice: Roy was deeply concerned about the societal injustices and inequalities that prevailed in India. He championed the cause of social reform and worked tirelessly to abolish practices such as sati (widow immolation), polygamy, and child marriage.

Educational Reform: Recognizing the importance of education in fostering social and intellectual progress, Roy was a strong advocate for modern education. He played a pivotal role in establishing schools that offered a blend of Indian and Western education.

Raja Ram Mohan Roy's religious reforms were instrumental in challenging orthodoxies and promoting a more inclusive and rational approach to spirituality. Some of his most significant contributions to religious reform include:

Critique of Idol Worship: Roy vehemently criticized the prevalent practice of idol worship in Hinduism. He argued that this practice contradicted the monotheistic essence of the religion and encouraged superstition. His critique paved the way for a more abstract and philosophical interpretation of Hinduism.

Defense of Monotheism: Roy authored several treatises, including "Tuhfat-ul-Muwahhidin" (Gift to Monotheists), in which he defended the concept of monotheism and emphasized the unity of God across various religious traditions.

Founding the Brahmo Samaj: In 1828, Raja Ram Mohan Roy founded the Brahmo Samaj, a socio-religious reform movement aimed at promoting monotheism, rationalism, and social reform. The Brahmo Samaj played a pivotal role in reshaping religious thought in India.

Advocacy for Religious Tolerance: Roy's advocacy for religious tolerance was a central theme in his writings and speeches. He believed in the coexistence of different religious traditions and actively worked to foster interfaith dialogue.

Translation of Scriptures: He translated the major Upanishads, the Vedanta, and the Rigveda into English and Persian, making the profound spiritual teachings of India accessible to a wider audience, including Western scholars.

Raja Ram Mohan Roy's commitment to social reform was driven by a deep concern for the plight of marginalized communities and the need to eradicate social evils. Some of the notable social reforms he championed include:

Abolition of Sati: Roy's relentless efforts played a crucial role in the eventual abolition of the practice of sati, whereby widows were compelled to self-immolate on their husband's funeral pyres. His influential work, "Sarvajanik Satya Dharma Pustak" (A Book on the True Religion for All), highlighted the irrationality and cruelty of sati.

Opposition to Child Marriage: He vociferously opposed the practice of child marriage, advocating for the legal age of marriage to be raised. His efforts contributed to the passage of laws aimed at curbing child marriages.

Women's Rights: Roy was an early advocate for women's rights and their education. He believed that women should have equal access to education and opportunities and should not be subjugated to oppressive customs.

Promoting Modern Education: Recognizing the importance of modern education in fostering social progress, Roy established schools that offered a blend of Western and Indian education. He believed that education was the key to enlightenment and societal reform.

Raja Ram Mohan Roy's contributions to Indian society, culture, and thought are immeasurable. His visionary ideas and tireless efforts continue to shape India's intellectual and social landscape. Here are some key aspects of his lasting legacy:

Promoter of Rationalism: Roy's emphasis on rationalism and critical thinking has had a profound and enduring impact on Indian intellectual discourse. His writings and teachings continue to inspire individuals and movements advocating for reason and scientific temper.

Advocate for Interfaith Harmony: His advocacy for religious tolerance and the unity of all religions laid the foundation for modern interfaith dialogue in India. His principles of religious pluralism and universal spirituality are still relevant in the context of India's diverse religious landscape.

Catalyst for Social Reform: Raja Ram Mohan Roy's tireless efforts in advocating for social reform led to significant changes in Indian society. The abolition of sati, opposition to child marriage, and his pioneering work in women's rights set the stage for future reform movements.

Founder of Brahmo Samaj: The Brahmo Samaj, founded by Roy, remains a prominent socio-religious organization that continues to promote his ideals of monotheism, rationalism, and social reform. It has played a crucial role in advancing religious and social thought in India.

Pioneer of Modern Education: His initiatives in education, including the establishment of schools, contributed to the spread of modern education in India. Today, his emphasis on education as a means of enlightenment and societal progress remains a guiding principle in the country.

Raja Ram Mohan Roy's life and work exemplify the spirit of reform and enlightenment that marked the Indian Renaissance. His visionary ideas, religious pluralism, and advocacy for rationalism continue to influence modern India.

As a champion of social justice, women's rights, and religious tolerance, he laid the groundwork for subsequent reform movements in India.

His legacy as the "Father of the Indian Renaissance" serves as an enduring source of inspiration for those who seek to build a just, inclusive, and enlightened society. Raja Ram Mohan Roy's commitment to the ideals of reason, social justice, and universal spirituality remains a beacon of hope and progress in the contemporary world.

RAJIV GANDHI

SHRI RAJIV GANDHI was born on August 20, 1944, in Bombay. His grandfather was the Indian independence leader Jawaharlal Nehru, who would become India's first Prime Minister after independence. His parents moved to New Delhi from Lucknow. His father, Feroze Gandhi, became an M.P., and earned a reputation as a fearless and hard-working Parliamentarian.

Rajiv Gandhi spent his early childhood with his grandfather in the Teen Murti House, where Indira Gandhi served as the Prime Minister's hostess. He briefly went to school at Welham Prep in Dehra Dun but soon moved to the residential Doon School in the Himalayan foothills. There he made many lifelong friendships and was also joined by his younger brother, Sanjay.

After leaving school, Shri Gandhi went to Trinity College, Cambridge, but soon shifted to the Imperial College (London). He did a course in mechanical engineering. He really was not interested in 'mugging for his exams', as went on to admit later.

It was clear that politics did not interest him as a career. According to his classmates, his bookshelves were lined with volumes on science and engineering, not works on philosophy, politics or history. Music, however, had a pride of place in his interests.

He liked Western and Hindustani classical, as well as modern music. Other interests included photography and amateur radio. His greatest passion, however, was flying. No wonder then, that on returning home from England, he passed the entrance examination to the Delhi Flying Club, and went to the obtain a commercial pilot's licence.

Soon, he became a pilot with Indian Airlines, the domestic national carrier. At Cambridge, he met and fell in love with an Italian student Sonia Maino, who was there to learn English. Sonia's family opposed the match, but Sonia came to India with Rajiv and they were married in 1968.

Gandhi began working for Indian Airlines as a professional pilot while his mother became Prime Minister in 1966. He exhibited no interest in politics and did not live regularly with his mother in Delhi at the Prime Minister's residence. In 1970, his wife, Sonia gave birth to Rahul, his first child, and in 1972, Priyanka, his second child and daughter. Theirs was a very private life despite the surrounding din and bustle of political activity.

But his brother Sanjay's death in an air crash in 1980 changed that. Pressures on Shri Gandhi to enter politics and help his mother, then besieged by many internal and external challenges, grew. He resisted these pressures at first, but later bowed to their logic. He won the by-election to the Parliament, caused by his brother's death, from Amethi in U.P.

In November 1982, when India hosted the Asian Games, the commitment made years earlier to build the stadia and other infrastructure was fulfilled. Shri Gandhi was entrusted with the task of getting all the work completed on time and ensuring that the games themselves were conducted without any hitches or flaws. In fulfilling this challenging task, he first displayed his flair for quiet efficiency and smooth coordination.

At the same time, as General Secretary of the Congress, he started streamlining and energising the party organisation with equal diligence. All these qualities came to the fore later in far more testing and trying times.

For no one could have ascended to power - becoming both Prime Minister and Congress President - in more tragic and tormenting circumstances than Shri Gandhi did in the wake of his mother's brutal assassination on 31 October, 1984. But he bore the awesome burden of personal grief and national responsibility with remarkable poise, dignity and restraint.

During the month long election campaign, Shri Gandhi travelled tirelessly from one part of the country to the other, covering a distance equal to one and a half times the earth's circumference, speaking at 250 meetings in as many places and meeting millions face to face.

A modern-minded, decisive but undemonstrative man, Shri Gandhi was at home in the world of high technology. And, as he repeatedly said, one of his main objectives, besides preserving India's unity, was to propel it into the twenty-first century.

Prime Minister Rajiv Gandhi began leading in a direction significantly different from Indira Gandhi's socialism. He improved bilateral relations with the United States - long strained owing to Indira's socialism and close friendship with the USSR - and expanded economic and scientific cooperation.

He increased government support for science and technology and associated industries, and reduced import quotas, taxes and tariffs on technology-based industries, especially computers, airlines, defence and telecommunications. He introduced measures significantly reducing the *License Raj* - allowing businesses and individuals to purchase capital, consumer goods and import without red-tape and bureaucratic restrictions.

In 1986, Rajiv announced a national education policy to modernize and expand higher education programs across India. Rajiv Gandhi was the founder of Jawahar Navodaya Vidyalaya System in the year 1986.

Rajiv Gandhi can be called the father of telecom revolution. His efforts created MTNL in 1986 and the public call offices, better known as PCOs, helped spread telephones in the rural areas. The work that he did then laid the foundation for a telecom boom in 1990s.

Rajiv authorized an extensive police and Army campaign to contain terrorism in Punjab. A state of martial law existed in the Punjab state, and civil liberties, commerce and tourism were greatly disrupted. There are many accusations of human rights violations by police officials as well as by the militants during this period.

It is alleged that even as the situation in Punjab came under control, the Indian government was offering arms and training to the LTTE rebels fighting the Government of Sri Lanka. The Indo-Sri Lanka Peace Accord was signed by Rajiv Gandhi and the Sri Lankan President J.R.Jayewardene, in Colombo on July 29, 1987.

The very next day, on July 30, 1987, Rajiv Gandhi was assaulted by a Sinhalese naval cadet named Vijayamunige Rohana de Silva, while receiving honor guard. Though the embarrassed Sri Lankan President J.R. Jayewardene initially attempted to pass off the bizarre assault as "Rajiv tripped a little and slightly lost his balance", Rajiv Gandhi while enroute to New Delhi asserted to J.N. Dixit who was in charge of arranging that disastrous visit, "What is all this nonsensical speculation. Of course, I was hit." Rajiv's government suffered a major setback when its efforts to arbitrate between the Government of Sri Lanka and the LTTE rebels backfired.

Rajiv's finance minister, Vishwanath Pratap Singh uncovered compromising details about government and political corruption, to the consternation of Congress leaders. Transferred to the Defence ministry, Singh uncovered what became known as the Bofors scandal, involving tens of millions of dollars - concerned alleged payoffs by the Swedish Bofors arms company through an Italian businessman and Gandhi family associate, Ottavio Quattrocchi, in return for Indian contracts.

Upon the uncovering of the scandal, Singh was conspicuously dismissed from office, and later from Congress membership. Rajiv Gandhi himself was later personally implicated in the scandal, when the investigation was continued by Narasimhan Ram and Chitra Subramaniam of *The Hindu* newspaper, shattering his image as an honest politician, however, he was cleared over this allegation in 2004. V. P. Singh's image as an exposer of government corruption made him very popular with the public, and opposition parties united under his name to form the Janata Dal coalition.

In the 1989 elections, the Congress suffered a major setback. With the support of Indian communists and the Bharatiya Janata Party, V. P. Singh and his Janata Dal formed a government. Rajiv Gandhi became the Leader of the Opposition, while remaining Congress president.

While some believe that Rajiv and Congress leaders influenced the collapse of V. P. Singh's government in 1990 by promising support to Chandra Shekhar, a high-ranking leader in the Janata Dal, sufficient internal contradictions existed, within the ruling coalition, especially over the controversial reservation issue, to cause a fall of government. Rajiv's Congress offered outside support briefly to Chandra Sekhar, who became Prime Minister. But this support was withdrawn in 1991 and fresh elections were announced.

The Indo-Sri Lanka Peace Accord signed was opposed by the then Sri Lankan Prime Minister Ranasinghe Premadasa and was forced to accept it due to pressure from then President Junius Richard Jayewardene. In January 1989 Premadasa was elected President and on a platform that promised that the Indian Peace Keeping Force (IPKF) leave within three months. In the 1989 elections both the Sri Lanka Freedom Party and United National Party wanted the IPKF to withdraw and they got 95% of the vote.

The police action was unpopular in India as well, especially in Tamil Nadu as India was fighting the LTTE Tamil separatists. Rajiv Gandhi refused to withdraw the IPKF, believing that the only way he could succeed in ending the civil war was to politically force Premadasa and militarily force the LTTE to accept the accord. Meanwhile in December 1989 Indian elections V.P.Singh became the Prime Minister and completed the pullout. The IPKF operation cost over 1100 Indian soldiers lives and cost over 2000 crores.

In 1985, Supreme court of India gave a judgement in favour of a Muslim divorcee Shah Banu that her husband should give alimony to her. Muslim fundamentalists in India treated it as an encroachment in Muslim Personal Law and protested against it.

Prime Minister, Rajiv Gandhi, agreed to their demands and cited the gesture as an example of "secularism". In 1986, the Congress (I) party, which had an absolute majority in Parliament at the time, passed an act that nullified the Supreme Court's judgment in the Shah Bano case.

The Shah Bano case generated tremendous heat in India. It proved that fundamentalist minorities can exert pressure on government and judicial decisions. The mainstream media disapproved of the decision. The opposition reacted strongly against the Congress party's policies (which, according to BJP, reflect "Pseudo-secularism".)

The case has led to Muslim women receiving a large, one-time payment from their husbands during the period of iddat, instead of a maximum monthly payment of 500 Rs (around 10 US dollars per month) - an upper limit which has since been removed. Cases of women getting lump sum payments for lifetime maintenance are becoming common.

Rajiv Gandhi's last public meeting was at Sriperumbudur on May 21, 1991, in a village approximately 30-miles from Chennai, Tamil Nadu, where he was assassinated while campaigning for the Sriperumbudur Lok Sabha Congress candidate. The Rajiv Gandhi Memorial was built at the site recently and is one of the major tourist attractions to the small industrial town.

SARDAR VALLABHBHAI PATEL

Sardar Patel was popularly known as Iron Man of India. His full name was Vallabhbhai Patel. He played a leading role in the Indian freedom struggle and became the first Deputy Prime Minister and Home Minister of India. He is credited with achieving political integration of India.

Vallabhbhai Patel was born on October 31, 1875 in Nadiad, a small village in Gujarat. His father Jhaverbhai was a farmer and mother Laad Bai was a simple lady. Sardar Vallabhai's early education took place in Karamsad.

Then he joined a school in Petlad. After two years he joined a high school in a town called Nadiad. He passed his high school examination in 1896. Sardar Vallabhbhai Patel was a brilliant student throughout his schooling.

Vallabhbhai wanted to become a barrister. To realize this ambition he had to go to England. But he did not have the financial means to even join a college India.

In those days a candidate could study in private and sit for an examination in Law. Sardar Vallabh Bhai Patel borrowed books from a lawyer of his acquaintance and studied at home. Occasionally he attended courts of law and listened attentively to the arguments of lawyer. Vallabhbhai passed the Law examination with flying colours.

Sardar Vallabhbhai Patel started his Law practice in Godhra. Soon his practice flourished. He got married to Jhaberaba. In 1904, he got a baby daughter Maniben, and in 1905 his son Dahyabhai was born.

Vallabhbhai sent his elder brother Vitthalbhai, who himself was a lawyer, to England for higher studies in Law. Patel was only thirty-three years old when his wife died.

He did not wish to marry again. After his brother's return, Vallabhbhai went to England. He studied with single-minded devotion and stood first in the Barrister-at-Law Examination.

Sardar Patel returned to India in 1913 and started his practice in Ahmedabad. Soon he became popular. At the urging of his friends, Patel contested and won elections to become the sanitation commissioner of Ahmedabad in 1917.

Sardar Patel was deeply impressed by Gandhiji's success in Champaran Satyagraha. In 1918, there was a drought in the Kheda division of Gujarat. Peasants asked for relief from the high rate of taxes but the British government refused. Gandhiji took up peasants cause but could not devote his full time in Kheda. He was looking for someone who could lead the struggle in his absence.

At this point Sardar Patel volunteered to come forward and lead the struggle. He gave up his lucrative legal practice and entered public life.

Vallabhbhai successfully led peasants revolt in Kheda and the revolt ended in 1919 when the British government agreed to suspend collection of revenue and roll back the rates. Kheda Satyagraha turned Vallabhbhai Patel into a national hero.

Vallabhbhai supported Gandhi's Non-Cooperation Movement, and as president of the Gujarat Congress, helped in organizing bonfires of British goods in Ahmedabad. He gave up his English clothes and started wearing Khadi. Sardar Vallabh Bhai Patel was elected Ahmedabad's municipal president in 1922, 1924 and 1927.

During his terms, Ahmedabad was extended a major supply of electricity and underwent major education reforms. Drainage and sanitation systems were extended over all the city.

In 1928, Bardoli Taluka in Gujarat suffered from floods and famine. In this hour of distress the British government raised the revenue taxes by thirty percent. Sardar Patel took up cudgels on behalf of the farmers and appealed to the Governor to reduce the taxes.

The Governor refused and the government even announced the date of the collection of the taxes. Sardar Patel organized the farmers and told them not to pay even a single pie of tax. The government tried to repress the revolt but ultimately bowed before Vallabhbhai Patel.

It was during the struggle and after the victory in Bardoli that caused intense excitement across India, that Patel was increasingly addressed by his colleagues and followers as Sardar.

Sardar Patel was imprisoned during Civil Disobedience Movement in 1930. After the signing of Gandhi-Irwin pact in 1931, Sardar Patel was released and he was elected Congress president for its 1931 session in Karachi.

Upon the failure of the Round Table Conference in London, Gandhiji and Sardar Patel were arrested in January 1932 and imprisoned in the Yeravada Central Jail.

During this term of imprisonment, Sardar Patel and Mahatma Gandhi grew close to one another, and the two developed a close bond of affection, trust, and frankness without reserve. Sardar Patel was finally released in July 1934.

In August 1942, the Congress launched the Quit India Movement. The government jailed all the important leaders of the Congress, including Vallabhai Patel.

All the leaders were released after three years. After achieving independence on 15th of August 1947, Pandit Jawaharlal Nehru became the first Prime Minister of independent India and Sardar Patel became the Deputy Prime Minister. He was in charge of Home Affairs, Information and Broadcasting and the Ministry of States.

There were 565 princely states in India at that time. Some of the Maharajas and Nawabs who ruled over these were sensible and patriotic. But most of them were drunk with wealth and power.

They were dreaming of becoming independent rulers once the British quit India. They argued that the government of free India should treat them as equals.

Some of them went to the extent of planning to send their representatives to the United Nations Organization.

Patel invoked the patriotism of India's monarchs, asking them to join in the freedom of their nation and act as responsible rulers who cared about the future of their people.

He persuaded the princes of 565 states of the impossibility of independence from the Indian republic, especially in the presence of growing opposition from their subjects. With great wisdom and political foresight, he consolidated the small kingdoms.

The public was with him. He tackled the Nizam of Hyderabad and the Nawab of Junagarh who initially did not want to join India.

Sardar Patel's untiring efforts towards the unity of the country brought success. He united a scattered nation without much bloodshed.

Due to the achievement of this massive task, Sardar Patel got the title of 'Iron Man'. Sardar Patel died of cardiac arrest on December 15, 1950. For his services to the nation Sardar Patel was conferred with Bharat Ratna in 1991.

SAROJINI NAIDU

Sarojini Naidu, the eldest daughter of scientist-philosopher, Aghornath Chattopadhyaya, and Barada Sundari Devi, a poetess was born on 13 February 1879 in Hyderabad. Her father was also a linguist, a crusader, who established the Nizam's College in Hyderabad in 1878, pioneering English and women's education.

Sarojini was a bright child who passed her matriculation at the age of 12 standing first in the Madras Presidency. She studied at the King's college, London and Girton College, Cambridge for a while. During this period her creative urge found expression in poems. She also happened to be a good singer. Her ability to sing charmingly fetched her the title 'Nightingale of India'. After 1917 she stepped into active politics. In 1898 she married Dr. Govindarajulu Naidu.

Her first volume of poetry, The Golden Threshold (1905), was followed by The Bird of Time (1912), and in 1914 she was elected a fellow of the Royal Society of Literature. Her collected poems, all of which she wrote in English, have been published under the titles The Sceptred Flute (1928) and The Feather of the Dawn (1961).

During 1903-17 Sarojini came into contact with Gokhale, Tagore, Jinnah, Annie Besant, C.P.Rama Swami Iyer, Gandhi and Nehru. She began her political career in 1906. From 1915 to 1918 she lectured all over India on welfare of youth, dignity of labour, women's emancipation and nationalism. After meeting Jawaharlal Nehru in 1916, she took up the cause of the indigo workers of Champaran. In 1925 she was elected as the President of the Congress.

Sarojini actively campaigned for the Montagu-Chelmsford Reforms, the Khilafat issue, the Rowlatt Act, the Sabarmati Pact, the Satyagraha Pledge and the Civil Disobedience Movement.

In 1919, she went to England as a member of the all-India home Rule Deputation. After 1920 she toured widely as the President of the Bombay Provincial Congress Committee opposed Council entry in Calcutta and protested against the anti-Moplah measures in Calicut.

From 1922-26 she espoused the cause of Indians in South Africa, she took part in the Salt Satyagraha and the Round Table Conference in London and campaigned for participation of women and youth in the public life. She organised a National Week in 1940 rallied against the Cripps Mission to India and was jailed in 1942 on the Quit India Resolution of the AICC in Bombay.

She was the first woman Governor of UP. Her Presidentship of the Asian Relations Conference in 1947 was remarkable. At the age of seventy on 02 March 1949 she died in office at Lucknow.

Sarojni Naidu married Govindarajalu Naidu, in 1898. Her daughter Padmaja Naidu was governor of West Bengal. Sarojini Naidu worked for women's rights, youth welfare, Hindu-Muslim unity throughout her life.

SHANKAR DAYAL SHARMA

Shankar Dayal Sharma (August 19 1918 - December 26 1999) was an Indian scholar and politician, most notable for serving as President of India from 1992 until 1997. He had previously served as President of the Indian National Congress. Shankar Dayal Sharma was married to Vimala Sharma.

Dr. Sharma received his education at St. John's College, Agra, Allahabad University, Lucknow University, Fitzwilliam College, Cambridge University, Lincoln's Inn and Harvard Law School. He took his M.A. Degrees in English Literature, Hindi and Sanskrit standing first in the University.

He obtained his LL.M. from Lucknow University once again standing first in the University. He obtained his Ph.D. in Law at Cambridge. Dr. Sharma was awarded the Chakravarti Gold Medal for Social Service by Lucknow University.

Dr. Sharma taught Law at Lucknow University and at Cambridge University. While at Cambridge, Dr. Sharma was Treasurer of the Tagore Society and the Cambridge Majlis.

Called to the Bar from Lincoln's Inn, he was later a Fellow at Harvard Law School. He has been elected Honorary Bencher and Master of Lincoln's Inn and Honorary Fellow, Fitzwilliam College, Cambridge. The University of Cambridge has honoured him with degree of Doctor of Law (Honoris Causa).

Dr. Sharma was Pro-Chancellor, Sagar University (1956-1959). During his tenure as Governor of Andhra Pradesh, Punjab and Maharashtra, he was Chancellor of 22 Universities in those States and also Rector of the University of Hyderabad.

During his tenure as Vice-President of India he was Chancellor of Delhi University, Punjab University, Pondicherry University, Gandhigram Rural Institute (Deemed University), and Visitor of Makhanlal Chaturvedi Rashtriya Patrakarita Vishwavidyalaya Sansthan, Bhopal. He was also Chairman of the Central Sanskrit Board.

Dr. Sharma was accorded the degree of Doctor of Laws (Honoris Causa) from (1) Vikram University; (2) Bhopal University; (3) Agra University; (4) Sri Venkateswara University, Tirupati; (5) Devi Ahilya Vishwavidyalaya, Indore and University of Sofia, Bulgaria.

He was also accorded the degree of Doctor of Social Sciences (Honoris Causa) from the University of roorkee, the degree of Doctor of Civil Law (Honoris Causa) from the University of

Mauritius (Port Louis), the degree of Doctor of Literature (Honoris Causa) from Meerut University, the degree of Doctorate (Honoris Causa) from Kiev State University, Ukraine, the degree of 'Vachaspati' from the Lal Bahadur Shastri Rashtriya Sanskrit Vidyapeeth (Deemed University), New Delhi, the degree of Doctorate (Honoris Causa) from Bucharest University, Romania, the degree of Doctor of Letters (Honoris Causa) from Agra University and the degree of 'Mahamahopadhyaya' (Honoris Causa) from the Rashtriya Sanskrit Vidyapeetha, Tirupati.

Dr. Sharma was President of: (i) Indian Council for Cultural Relations, New Delhi; and (ii) Indian Institute of Public Administration, New Delhi, and Chairman of: (i) the Jury for the Jawaharlal Nehru Award for International Understanding, and (ii) the International Jury for the Indira Gandhi Prize for Peace, Disarmament and Development.

Dr. Sharma started his legal practice in 1940 in Lucknow. Dr. Sharma participated in the historic Quit India Movement during the national struggle for freedom, and in the merger Movement in Bhopal, and underwent imprisonments.

Dr. Sharma was Chief Minister of the erstwhile Bhopal State (1952-1956), Cabinet Minister, Government of Madhya Pradesh, holding the portfolios of Education, Law, Public Works, Industry and Commerce, National Resources and Separate Revenue (1956-1967) and was thereafter Union Minister for Communications (1974-1977).

Dr. Sharma was Vice-President of India and Chairman of the Council of States (Rajya Sabha) from September 3, 1987 till he assumed office of the President of India in 1992. Earlier he has been the Governor of three States: Andhra Pradesh, Punjab and Maharashtra.

Dr. Sharma was President of the (i) Bhopal Congress Committee (1950-52) and (ii) Madhya Pradesh Congress Committee (1967-68): General Secretary, Indian National Congress (1968-72); Member, (i) All India Congress Committee for more than 32 years (1952-84) and (ii) Congress Working Committee for about 20 years. Dr. Sharma was the President of the Indian National Congress in 1972-1974.

Dr. Sharma was Member, Bhopal Legislative Assembly (1952-1956); Madhya Pradesh Legislative Assembly (1956-1971); Fifth Lok Sabha (1971-1977) and Seventh Lok Sabha (1980-1984). His participation in matters concerning Parliament was resumed when he assumed office as Vice-President of India and ex-officio Chairman of the Council of State (Rajya Sabha), and continues in his office as President of India.

Dr. Sharma led several official delegations to International Conferences including a Parliamentary Delegation to the Inter-Parliamentary Union Conference at Oslo in 1980; a Special Delegation of veteran freedom fighters to Moscow in August, 1987 for the celebrations of the 40th Anniversary of India's Independence during the Festival of India in USSR, also led a Special Delegation of veteran freedom fighters to Jalalabad (Afghanistan) to pay homage to Khan Abdul Ghaffar Khan in 1988.

The title of 'Bharat Ratnam' (Jewel of the Nation) has been conferred upon Dr. Sharma by His Holiness the Shankaracharya of Sringeri. The title of "Dharmaratnakara' has been conferred on him by the Pontiff of Shravanbelagola.

The International Bar Association has presented to Dr. Sharma the Living Legends of Law Award of Recognition for his outstanding contribution to the legal profession internationally and for commitment to the Rule of Law.

Reading and writing on various subjects of national and international interest and study of languages, history, art and culture, comparative religion, philosophy, poetry, literature and classical Indian and Western music.

During the 1960s Sharma supported Indira Gandhi's quest for leadership of the Congress Party. He served in her cabinet as the minister for Communication from 1974-77.

Later on, he was given a variety of ceremonial posts. In 1984 he began serving as a governor of Indian states, first in Andhra Pradesh. During this time, his daughter and son-in-law were killed by Sikh militants.

In 1985 he left Andhra Pradesh and became governor of Punjab during a time of violence between the Indian government and Sikh militants, many of whom lived in Punjab. He left Punjab in 1986 and took up his final governorship in Maharashtra. He remained governor of that state until 1987 when he was elected for a 5-year term as Vice-President of India and chairman of the Rajya Sabha.

Sharma was known to be a stickler for parliamentary norms. He is known to have broken down in the Rajya Sabha while witnessing the members of the house create a din on a political issue. His grief brought back some order into the proceedings of the house.

Sharma served as Vice-President until 1992, when he was elected President. After a difficult campaign, he received 66% of the votes in the electoral college, defeating George Swell.

During his five-year term, he was active in ceremonial matters and was in charge of dismissing and appointing governors.

During his last year as President, it was his responsibility to swear in three prime ministers. He did not run for a second term as President.

During the last five years of his life, Sharma suffered from ill health. On October 9 1999, he suffered a massive heart attack and was admitted to a hospital in New Delhi, where he died. He was cremated near the Vijay Ghat.

SHYAMA PRASAD MUKHERJI

Shyama Prasad Mukherji (1901-1953) scholar, Hindu nationalist and parliamentarian. Shyama Prasad Mukherji was born on 6 July 1901 in a Brahmin family of a high social status in Calcutta. From his parents, Sir asutosh mookerjee and Shrimati Jogmaya Devi, he inherited a saga of erudite scholarship and fervent nationalism. They also inspired him to 'live a pure and manly life'.

Graduating in 1921 with Honours in English and securing the first position in the first class from the Presidency College, Shyama Prasad Mukherji had his MA in Indian Vernaculars. Then he got a BL degree in 1924 and topped the list in the Calcutta University.

Since his student days, Shyama Prasad assisted his vice-chancellor father in forming the educational plans. After his father's death in 1924, his presence at the University Senate and Syndicate was considered essential. In 1934, he became the youngest Vice-Chancellor of the university.

Shyama Prasad's political career was also characterised by high idealism. In 1929 he was elected to the Bengal Legislative Council as a Congress candidate from the university constituency.

He acted as a safeguard for the university in the council. But, in response to the Congress call for boycott of councils, he resigned but later re-entered it as an independent member for the sake of the university. In 1937 he was re-elected from the university constituency.

The passing of the Secondary Education and the Calcutta University Bills seriously impaired the educational structure of Bengal. Shyama Prasad endeavoured to persuade the Congress leadership to topple the ministry, but failed.

He, therefore, rallied round himself non-Congress and non-Muslim League nationalist forces and formed the coalition ministry with ak fazlul huq as the Chief Minister and himself shouldering the Ministry of Finance. During this period Veer Savarkar created a deep impression on him and he joined the hindu mahasabha and became its acting president in 1939.

When the quit india movement started, the British unleashed a reign of terror in the country and all the Congress leaders were put in to jail. In fact, there was no one to take up the national cause. Shyama Prasad, though a member of the government, voluntarily took up his national responsibilities.

Having failed to persuade the central government to desist from its repressive measures, he decided to quit the Bengal Cabinet and to lead the national forces against the British.

During the 1943 famine, his humanitarian work saved a lot of lives. Soon after the rigorous famine the shadow of partition began to threaten the stability of life. He put forward the argument that if at all India was to be partitioned on the communal basis, in that case Bengal and Punjab must be partitioned on the same ground.

Here also Shyama Prasad stood firm and swam against the partition current. In the complex political scenario, his endeavour went in vain. Shyama Prasad joined the first government of free India as Minister for Industries and supplies.

But his difference with Nehru led to his resignation from the ministry. He became the first member of the opposition in the Parliament and Constituent Assembly of India. He concentrated his energy to create a real democratic opposition.

The result was the Bharatiya Jana Sangha. In the first general election Jana Sangha was only able to send three members, including Shyama Prasad to the first Lok Sabha. Though he had limited members, but together with other small parties, he formed the National Democratic Party in the Parliament, of which he was elected leader. His role in the Lok Sabha as the leader of opposition earned him the title 'lion of Parliament'. In 1953, he died in Srinagar.

SIR SYED AHMED KHAN

Syed Ahmed was born in Delhi, 1817. Ghalib was twenty year old at that time, and a close family friend. Syed Ahmed, as he was growing up, began calling him 'Chacha Ghalib' (or Uncle Ghalib) out of fondness, and the title stuck on the poet forever.

Syed Ahmed's father, Mir Taqi (not to be confused with the poet), was a mystic who shied away from participating in the affairs of the world, leaving them all up to his father-in-law. He died when Syed Ahmed was twenty-one, but seems to have left little impact on him.

Mother, Azizunnissa Begum was, however, a woman of clearly defined views and inexhaustible energies. There is a famous story about how the young Syed Ahmed was kicked out of the house by his mother for hitting an old servant. He was admitted back only through intermediation of some relatives, and after he had duly asked forgiveness from the servant.

The Mughal society of Delhi was a rigidly class-based structure, and Azizunnisa Begum's outrage at her son's abuse of a poor servant might well have been due to the teachings of such reformers as Shah Abdul Aziz (the first translator of the Holy Quran into Urdu), of whom she was a devout follower.

However, Syed Ahmed learnt only half his lesson: while he persistently showed respect for humanity, he nevertheless failed to gain control over his hot temper. To the end of his days he was known for his cataclysmic outbursts of anger. Syed Ahmed was only nine when Ghalib undertook the arduous journey from Delhi to Calcutta.

On his return, he was a changed man. Quite contrary to how Mr. Naseeruddin Shah was going to depict him on the screen one hundred and seventy-five years later (courtesy Gulzar), the historical Ghalib was all praise for the able administration of the British, and would fondly describe how the streets of Calcutta, the British Capital in India, were neatly maintained and designed to an order.

Syed himself wasn't much interested in studies in the beginning (and he never mastered the English language to the end). According to his own admission, he was briefly drawn to the usual pleasures of those days, such as listening to music and watching dance. Life changed upon the death of his father.

Syed was forced to seek the dual employment of the Mughal Court and the British East India Company. This was a common practice in those last days of the Mughal Empire, since the King himself was living off on a regular pension from the British. A "royal employment" would quite often mean nothing more than an impressive title – Jawwaduddaula Arif-e-Jang, or The Overseer of the Kingdom, The Sage of War, in the case of Syed Ahmed!

Syed Ahmed was forty when the upheaval of 1857 took place. Until then, he was torn between his nostalgia for the Mughal past and his admiration for the Western thought.

His elder brother was a journalist, and from his press Syed Ahmed used to publish books about the former grandeur of the Mughals. One of these was Asarus Sanadid, an exhaustive study of the architectural heritage of Delhi.

He literally risked his life while documenting inscriptions written on the ceilings of dilapidated buildings. It is said that he worked so hard that he seriously fell ill. Another was a thoroughly revised edition of Ain-e-Akbari (a medieval treatise on the government in the days of Akbar the Great).

For this later effort, he received a frank rebuke from Uncle Ghalib in fluid Persian poetry: Ghalib urged his nominal nephew to wake up to the new age that had begun to dawn. Any effort to recall the glory of the Mughals, according to Ghalib, was "an effort in futility." Syed Ahmed was still not so sure of that.

But what happened in the fateful summer of 1857 shook him to the core of his conscience. Today, many historians describe it as The War of Independence, but that wasn't how Syed Ahmed, Mirza Ghalib, and other enlightened Indians of the times looked at it.

To them, it was a conspiracy by backward looking forces to push their country back into the medieval times, and stop the advancement of rational thought.

At the very outset of the revolt, the rebel leaders started killing every white man, woman or children that they could lay their hands on.

Syed Ahmed was posted at Bijnour at that time. He risked his own life to save a British family from the hands of the freedom fighters. At one point, the fighters besieged his bungalow, demanding that he should hand over the refugees to them.

Syed Ahmed resisted with an unmatched courage, something he was to display many times again in his life when pitched against the fanatics. Later, when the British Government offered him a huge estate in reward, he refused it. He had acted from conviction, not for reward.

Meanwhile, the freedom fighters at Delhi had issued a proclamation in the name of a Mughal prince, in which they outlined how they intended to rule the country once the British were ousted.

They listed the cruelties committed by the British infidels, such as that "on the complaint of a common peasant, a maidservant, or a slave, the respectable landlords are summoned into court, arrested, put into jail and thus disgraced."

The freedom fighters promised that when they come into power, they would stop such atrocities, and "every landlord will have absolute rule over his property." The idea of restoring the local monarchy over the Sub-Continent by overthrow of the British might have been a beautiful dream for some, but it was most certainly the worst nightmare of people like Ghalib and Syed Ahmed.

After the recapture of Delhi by the British army, Syed Ahmed went back to rescue Azizunnisa Begum, now a helpless old lady. There, he must have seen the fruits of the British revenge: it is said that for several miles outside Delhi the trees were strewn with the corpses of the citizens of Delhi, who were hanged on them after a summary trial.

This scene, which was described countless times over the next hundred years to move sentimental patriotic crowds into a frenzy against the British Raj, failed to sway the rational judgment of Syed Ahmed even as he was looking at the ruins of Delhi – the ancient buildings he had documented with so much passion all turned into rubble now. But he was a historian, and he remembered that the earlier conquerors of Delhi had also allowed their armies to plunder.

The massacre by the armies of Nadir Shah, just a little over a century ago, was perhaps just as bad as what was now lying in front of Syed Ahmed. The raids of the Marhattas, in their days of power, would culminate in ghastly scenes too. The British storming of Delhi was brutal mainly by the British standards. By the standards of the Indian history, it was just like many other captures of Delhi.

This is almost exactly what Syed Ahmed wrote in his account of the Revolt, which was published under the title, *Tarikh Sarkashi-e-Zila Bijnour.* "In India, people are not at all used to learn about former times from the facts of history, nor from reading books," he lamented.

"It is for this reason that you people are not familiar with the injustice and oppression that used to take place in the days of the past rulers." Mirza Ghalib had already denounced the War of Independence (then known as the Mutiny) as "rustakheez-e-beja," or a "Rebellion without a Cause," which formed the subtitle of his own account of the uprising.

Syed Ahmed has been most misunderstood from this point

onwards. While his detractors present him as a partisan of the British government, his defenders do him no less harm by maintaining that Syed Ahmed's main concern was only the interests of his own community, for which purpose he feigned loyalty to the British Crown.

The truth is that Syed Ahmed was far above either of these concerns. He was a rationalist, first and last. The uprising of 1857 had jolted him up to proclaim that the human beings can only be divided into two classes: those who listen to logic, and those who don't.

Only those who can use their rational faculty and rise above sentiments are capable of making ethical decisions.

In 1869, when Syed Ahmed went to London, he found a big chunk of the puzzle he was trying to solve. In a letter from there, he wrote, "Look at this young girl Elizabeth Matthews (a housemaid where he was staying), who, in spite of her poverty, invariably buys a half-penny paper called the "Echo" and reads it when at leisure... Cabmen and coachmen keep a paper or a book under their seats and after taking the passenger to his destination, or in case the coach has to wait, they take out their newspaper and start reading."

With an increased conviction than before, Syed Ahmed concluded that, "Unless the education of the masses is pushed on in India, as it is here, it is impossible for a native to become civilized and honored." However, Syed Ahmed was not one to tone down his words once he was sure that he was speaking the truth.

"Without flattering the English," he wrote in the same letter. "I can truly say that the natives of India, high and low... when contrasted with the English in education, manners, and uprightness, are as like them as a dirty animal is to an able and andsome man." It seems that the angry young boy who had struck t his servant with anger still remained unbroken somewhere nside.

n that same journey, the honorific of KCSI was bestowed upon yed Ahmed, which entitled him to prefix his name with "Sir." Hence he became "Sir Syed" from that point onwards. By that ime he was the most prominent Muslim in India.

Ie had penned down a series of comparative studies on Christianity and Islam, emphasizing similarities rather than ifferences between the two; he had established schools; he had lso founded a society for the advancement of scientific thought, vhose main function was to translate treatises on modern science rom the European languages into Urdu.

Iowever, his greatest achievements were yet to come – his famous eriodical *Tehzeebul Akhlaq* in 1872, and the establishment of the Mohammedan Anglo-Oriental School at Aligarh (which became college in 1877 and was inaugurated by the Viceroy). Much has een written on these accounts.

But what has often gone unnoticed is that the objectives of Sir yed were not so much aimed along the communal lines (special rovisions were made at Aligarh College for accommodating Hindu students, and Sir Syed generally preached that Muslims hould refrain from slaughtering cows on the Eid), as they were long the divide of the rational faculty versus common sentiment.

ir Syed is most misunderstood in his opposition to the Indian National Congress, which was founded in 1885. It is said that he pposed it mainly out of a fear of the Hindu domination. Even f that may be true, it cannot be more than a half-truth. The omplete truth, as may be gathered from his own writings (quite asily available), is that Sir Syed opposed the Congress because it vas heading towards politics.

He feared that any kind of politics in India would invariably resor to religious sentiments. This, in the opinion of Sir Syed, woulc disrupt the harmony, which he wanted to preserve abov everything else. Mentioning the ideas of John Stuart Mill or representative government, he declared: "The aims and object of the Indian National Congress are based upon an ignorance o history and present-day realities." A utilitarian individualist of th same school of thought as Mill, he was of the opinion that th main purpose of a responsible government was to ensure persona liberties and maximum happiness for the individual.

He had no time for totalitarian movements that asked for sacrifice in the name of abstract ideals. "I consider the experiment whicl the Indian National Congress wants to make fraught with danger and sufferings for all the nationalities of India, specially for th Muslims," he declared in his characteristic matter of fact style.

You could hate him, or you could love him, but he would neve give you words that could be interpreted in two different ways "The Muslims are in minority, but...at least traditionally they ar prone to take the sword in hand when the majority oppresse them. If this happens, it will bring about disaster greater than th ones which came in the wake of the happenings of 1857."

Indeed, he was not expressing his heartfelt desire, but only hi worst suspicions. Quite prophetically, this came true in th bloodshed of 1947. But nobody by that time was in a mind t remember the voice of reason that he had tried to infuse into hi people. The Hindus had given up the ideals of the Brahmo Sama and the Muslims had reverted back to that starry-eyed nostalgi against which Sir Syed had repeatedly warned them.

Of course there were a thousand variables involved, and thousand different ways to explain what followed between Si Syed's death in 1898, and the inception of two independent state in 1947, but if he were to come back on the eve of freedom, perhaps his only question to the two emerging nations would have been, "In what manner have you prepared yourselves?" And he, indeed, was the last man who could be satisfied with any answer that smacked of sentiments. This great scholar and leader died on 27th March, 1898, at Aligarh, India.

SONIA GANDHI

Sonia Gandhi was born in Ovassanjo, 80 km away from Turin Italy on December 9, 1946. She born into a family of modest means in an Italian village on the banks of a river 57 years ago Sonia Maino, now Sonia Gandhi, has weaved a dramatic way to a place in history by becoming the President of India's century-old Congress party.

Being the third woman of foreign origin to hold the prestigious post after Annie Beasant and Nelli Sengupta, Sonia Gandhi also became the fifth from the Nehru family to take over the Congress reins. The other four were Motilal Nehru, Jawaharlal Nehru, Indira Gandhi and Rajiv Gandhi.

She also is the eighth person of the foreign origin to be the Congress president. On 28th May 2005 Smt. Sonia Gandhi was elected as President of the Indian National Congress by overwhelming support from across the country from all states.

In a short span since she plunged into active politics before the February mid-term Lok Sabha elections, Sonia in fact, had wrought a political miracle by becoming the dual chief of the 113 year old Indian National Congress and its Parliamentary party.

In the process, Sonia Gandhi also emulated her husband, mother-in-law and grandfather-in-law—Rajiv, Indira and Nehru— who all held the two posts during their career.

Since Rajiv's death, Sonia had led a life of near recluse for six years but for her appearances at a few official functions. She touched many a heart when she poured out her 'vedna' (agony) at a public meeting a few years ago in Amethi about the delay in the probe of Rajiv assassination case.

Barring such vieled political statements, Sonia hid her emotions behind a thick veil of secrecy keeping observers guessing about whether she nursed political intentions at all.

But fawning Congressmen, looking for a charismatic personality to lead the party to electoral success, kept sending their appeals to her to come and take over the party.

After an excruciating spell of suspense, Sonia, who long remained something of an enigma to many, finally decided to campaign for the Congress in the just-concluded Lok Sabha electors and is credited by observers with preventing a doom for the party. Congress, which was forecast not to cross the double digit mark managed a tally of 141 seats, largely due to her charismatic presence during the campaign.

In fact, the top job of the Congress organisation was offered to her on a platter immediately after the death of her husband on May 21, 1991. But a grieving and reluctant Sonia declined the offer. Travelling the length and breadth of the country in a hurricane election tour, Sonia caught the imagination of the masses, by her emotional speeches in Hindi prepared in advance.

Observers commented that Sonia successfully adopted her mother-in-law's mannerism and style in warming her way to large crowds which had turned up at her election rallies. Sonia, whose Italian origin gave her opponents propaganda grist became a full-fledged Indian citizen in 1984 after the death of Indira Gandhi.

Sonia met Rajiv Gandhi in Cambridge during 1960s when the former Prime Minister was studying at the famous British University. They were married in 1968 after three years of courtship which began in a Greek restaurant in the university town. The simple ceremony was held on Vasant Panchami day in February, the same day when Indira Gandhi married Feroze decades earlier.

The wedding was a simple nondenominational ceremony in the garden of 1, Safdarjang Road. Sonia wore a pink sari made from cotton which Nehru had spun while in prison... It was the same sari which Indira had worn for her wedding, says biographer Nicholas Nugent in his book Rajiv Gandhi —son of a dynasty.

Eventually, Rajiv resigned from Indian Airlines to join politics after Sanjay's death in 1980. That was history. Now not only Sonia is in the thick of politics, but her children, Rahul and Priyanka, too are in great demand in the Congress circle for taking over the Youth Congress.

VEER SAVARKAR

Veer Savarkar occupies a unique place in the history of Indian freedom struggle. His name evokes controversy. While some consider him as one of the greatest revolutionaries in the Indian freedom struggle, others consider him a communalist and Machiavellian manipulator. Vir Savarkar was also a great orator, prolific writer, historian, poet, philosopher and social worker.

He was an extraordinary Hindu scholar. He coined Indian words for telephone, photography, the parliament, among others. Veer Savarkar's original name was Vinayak Damodar Savarkar.

He was born on May 28, 1883 in the village of Bhagur near Nasik. He was one among four children born to Damodarpant Savarkar and Radhabai. Veer Savarkar had his initial education at the Shivaji School, Nasik. He lost his mother when he was only nine. Savarkar was a born rebel. He organized a gang of kids ,Vanarsena when he was just eleven.

During his high school days, Veer Savarkar used to organize Shivaji Utsav and Ganesh Utsav, started by Bal Gangadhar Tilak (whom Savarkar considered as his Guru) and used these occasions to put up plays on nationalistic themes. Savarkar lost his father during the plague of 1899.

In March 1901, he married Yamunabai. Post marriage, in 1902, Veer Savarkar joined Fergusson College in Pune.

In Pune, Savarkar founded the "Abhinav Bharat Society". He was also involved in the Swadeshi movement and later joined Tilak's Swaraj Party. His instigating patriotic speeches and activities incensed the British Government. As a result the British Government withdrew his B.A. degree.

In June 1906, Veer Savarkar, left for London to become Barrister. However, once in London, he united and inflamed the Indian students in England against British rule in India. He founded the Free India Society.

The Society celebrated important dates on the Indian calendar including festivals, freedom movement landmarks, and was dedicated to furthering discussion about Indian freedom.

He believed and advocated the use of arms to free India from the British and created a network of Indians in England, equipped with weapons.

In 1908, brought out an authentic informative researched work on The Great Indian Revolt, which the British termed as "Sepoy Mutiny" of 1857. The book was called "The Indian War of Independence 1857".

The British government immediately enforced a ban on the publication in both Britain and India. Later, it was published by Madame Bhikaiji Cama in Holland, and was smuggled into India to reach revolutionaries working across the country against British rule.

In 1909, Madanlal Dhingra, a keen follower of Savarkar shot Sir Wyllie after a failed assassination attempt on the then Viceroy, Lord Curzon. Savarkar conspicuously did not condemn the act.

When the then British Collector of Nasik, A.M.T. Jackson was shot by a youth, Veer Savarkar finally fell under the net of the British authorities. He was implicated in the murder citing his connections with India House. Savarkar was arrested in London on March 13, 1910 and sent to India.

After a formal trial, Savarkar was charged with serious offences of illegal transportation of weapons, provocative speeches and sedition and was sentenced to 50 years' of jail and deported to the Kalapani (Blackwaters) at Andaman cellular jail.

In 1920, many prominent freedom fighters including Vithalbhai Patel, Mahatma Gandhi and Bal Gangadhar Tilak demanded the release of Savarkar.

On May 2, 1921, Savarkar was moved to Ratnagiri jail, and from there to the Yeravada jail. In Ratnagiri jail Savarkar wrote the book 'Hindutva'. On January 6, 1924 he was then freed under the condition that he would not leave Ratnagiri district and abstain from political activity for the next five years.

On his release, Veer Savarkar founded the Ratnagiri Hindu Sabha on January 23, 1924 that aimed to preserve India's ancient culture and work for social welfare.

Later Savarkar joined Tilak's Swaraj Party and founded the Hindu Mahasabha as a separate political party. He was elected President of the Mahasabha and toiled for building Hindu Nationalism and later joined the Quit India movement.

The Hindu Mahasabha opposed creation of Pakistan, and took exception to Gandhi's continued Muslim appeasement stances. Nathuram Godse, a volunteer of the Hindu Mahasabha, assassinated Gandhi in 1948 and upheld his actions till his hanging.

Veer Savarkar was arrested and indicted by the Government of India in the Mahatma Gandhi assassination case. But he was acquitted by the Supreme Court of India, for reasons of lack of evidence. Veer Savarkar died on February 26, 1966 at the age of 83.

VIJAYA LAKSHMI PANDIT

Vijaya Lakshmi Pandit was born on Aug. 18, 1900, Allahabad, India and she died on Dec. 1, 1990, Dehra Dun. Indian political leader and diplomat, one of the world's leading women in public life in the 20th century. She was active in the Indian freedom movement and held high national and international positions.

Vijaya Lakshmi Pandit was born in Allahabad in what was then the United Provinces (later, Uttar Pradesh) on August 18, 1900, and was given the name Swarup Kumari ("Beautiful Princess") Nehru. She was the eldest daughter of a distinguished Brahmin lawyer, Motilal Nehru, and eleven years younger than her brother, Jawaharlal.

Accustomed to luxury and educated at home and in Switzerland, she was greatly influenced by Mohandas Gandhi and became identified with the struggle for independence. She was imprisoned by the British on three different occasions, in 1932-1933, 1940, and 1942-1943.

In May 1921 she married Ranjit Sitaram Pandit, a foreign-educated barrister from Kathiawar. At that time she changed her name to Vijaya Lakshmi Pandit. The Pandit's had three daughters, including the novelist Nayantara (Pandit) Sehgal. Her husband died on January 14, 1944.

In 1934 Pandit's long career in politics officially began with her election to the Allahabad Municipal Board.

In 1936 she was elected to the Assembly of the United Provinces, and in 1937 became minister of local self-government and public health—the first Indian woman ever to become a cabinet minister. Like all Congress party officeholders, she resigned in 1939 to protest against the British government's declaration that India was a participant in World War II. Along with other Congress leaders, she was imprisoned after the Congress' "Quit India" Resolution of August 1942.

Forced to reorient her life after her husband's death, Pandit traveled in the United States from late 1944 to early 1946, mainly on a lecture tour.

Vijaya Lakshmi Nehru Pandit (1900 - 1990) was an Indian diplomat and politician, sister of Indian Prime Minister Jawaharlal Nehru, and the first female President of the United Nations General Assembly.

In 1921 she married Ranjit Sitaram Pandit. She was the first Indian woman to hold a cabinet post. In 1937 she was elected to the provincial legislature of the United Provinces and designated minister of local self-government and public health. She held the latter post until 1939 and again from 1946 to 1947.

Following India's independence from the British in 1947, she entered the diplomatic service and became India's ambassador to several different countries: the Soviet Union from 1947 to 1949, the United States and Mexico from 1949 to 1951, Ireland from 1955 to 1961 (during which time she was also the Indian High Commissioner to the United Kingdom), and Spain from 1958 to 1961. Between 1946 and 1968 she also headed the Indian delegation to the United Nations.

In India, she served as governor of Maharashtra from 1962 until 1964, after which she was elected to the Indian Lok Sabha from Phulpur, her brother's former constituency. She held office from 1964 to 1968. Pandit was a harsh critic of her niece, Indira Gandhi, after Gandhi became Prime Minister in 1966, and she retired from active politics after relations soured between them.

In 1979 she was appointed the Indian representative to the UN Human Rights Commission, after which she retired from public life. Her writings include The Evolution of India (1958) and The Scope of Happiness: A Personal Memoir (1979). Her daughter Nayantara Sehgal is a well-known novelist.

Returning to India in January 1946, she resumed her portfolio as minister of local self-government and public health in the United Provinces. In the fall of 1946 she undertook her first official diplomatic mission as leader of the Indian delegation to the United Nations General Assembly. She also led India's delegations to the General Assembly in 1947, 1948, 1952, 1953, and 1963.

Pandit was elected to India's Constituent Assembly in 1946. Shortly after India's independence in 1947, she joined the foreign service and was appointed India's first ambassador to the Soviet Union. In early 1949 she became ambassador to the United States.

In November 1951 she returned to India to contest successfully for a seat in the Lok Sabha in the first general elections. In September 1953 she was given the honor of being the first woman and the first Asian to be elected president of the U.N. General Assembly.

For nearly seven years, beginning in December 1954, Pandit served as Indian high commissioner (ambassador) to the United Kingdom, including a tense period in British-Indian relations at the time of the Suez and Hungarian crisis' in 1956. From March 1963 until August 1963 she served as governor of the state of Maharashtra.

Jawaharlal Nehru's death on May 27, 1964 came as a great shock to her. In November, she was elected to the Lok Sabha in a by-election in the Phulpur constituency of Uttar Pradesh, which her brother had represented for 17 years. She was re-elected in the fourth general elections in 1967, but resigned the following year for "personal reasons."

Furious at Indira Gandhi's (whose maiden name was Nehru) state-of-emergency suspension of democratic processes from 1975 to 1977, she campaigned against her niece. Her efforts resulted in an electoral defeat for Gandhi.

Pandit had not been politically active for several years when she died in Dehru Dun, India on December 1, 1990. On the occasion of her death, President Ramaswami Venkataraman described Pandit as a "luminous strand in the tapestry of India's freedom struggle. Distinctive in her elegance, courage, and dedication, Mrs. Pandit was an asset to the national movement."

~~~
~~~